OK Sierra
A Drama in Three Acts

Performance rights must be secured before production. All rights for this play are owned by Adam Nathaniel Davis. He can be contacted through his website (http://writing.voyage), via email (adam@writing.voyage), or by phone (904-434-9210).

MAIN CHARACTERS (REQUIRED)

DAVIN	A financial trader whose life has been in disarray over the last several years
SIERRA & SONYA	Davin's AIde – a digital assistant that lives inside his brain
LOREN	Davin's manager at the trading firm
RODERICK	One of Davin's good friends and a colleague on his team at the trading firm
SKYA	A woman that Davin begins dating
SHANNON	An installation technician for Integrated Intelligence

MINOR CHARACTERS (DOUBLING POSSIBLE)

NOVIA	Roderick's AIde
LEON	Loren's AIde
MAX	Skya's AIde
WAITER	Present during Act Three, Scene One

NOTES FROM THE WRITER

This play is set in the not-too-distant future and much of it focuses on the interaction between people and their AIdes. An AIde is a digital assistant implanted directly into the base of a person's brain. The person can hear the voice of the AIde, but does not see any physical manifestation of the assistant. AIdes have direct access to a wide array of public resources and are much more powerful than today's computers. They are ubiquitous throughout society and are an integral part of each person's existence. The hardware for each AIde exists in a small black box affixed to the back of everyone's neck. Every character that is not an AIde should have one of these boxes on their neck.

Because they are not seen, an AIde should not be physically addressed by its host. Someone interacting with their AIde will look as though they are talking to themselves (e.g. like someone talking into a Bluetooth ear piece). On stage, the AIde could be represented by an actor wearing black-or-muted clothing and standing *behind* the host. AIdes do not exist in physical space. Their presence on stage is solely to serve as a visual representation of the conversations taking place between AIdes and their hosts. Each AIde can only be heard by its host. So when an AIde speaks, no other characters – other than the AIde's host – should be reacting directly to those words.

It's feasible that all of the AIdes except Sierra could have their lines delivered over a sound system. This would highlight the fact that they are not as advanced as Sierra and it would cut down on casting requirements for the other AIdes.

It's vital that the AIdes do _not_ speak in stilted or monotone patterns, stereotypical of outdated computer clichés. AIdes speak in human tones. They are capable of a wide array of inflection that mimics all aspects of human language. They don't sound like computers. They sound like people. They are not simply computer programs. They are artificial intelligences. Their voices feature varying pitch, tone, *and emotion*.

AIdes are programmed with gender-specific personas. Men typically have "female" AIdes, and women typically have "male" AIdes.

The play is race neutral. Davin (or any other character) could be played by a black/asian/latino/whatever actor just as well as a white actor. Even the genders of the characters are somewhat malleable. For example, Loren is written as female, but could easily be changed to male. The issues addressed in the play are mostly race/gender neutral.

The play is written to cater to minimalist set design. Although more elaborate sets would not take away from the production, the action in the play should not require much extravagance.

ACT ONE, SCENE ONE

(THE STAGE IS COMPLETELY DARK.)

SIERRA: Wake up, Davin.

(A SPOTLIGHT SHINES ON A SMALL PORTION OF DAVIN'S BEDROOM. HE SLOWLY RISES FROM BED.)

SIERRA: (SPOKEN AS DAVIN FUMBLES THROUGH HIS MORNING ROUTINE) The Scorpions beat the Cougars last night 93 to 89. This forces game seven in the series, which will be played Saturday night in Marmont. The latest polls—

DAVIN: OK Sierra.

(THERE IS AN ABRUPT PAUSE AS SIERRA AWAITS INSTRUCTIONS.)

DAVIN: (WHILE DRESSING) What is the point spread?

SIERRA: The Cougars are favored by three-and-a-half.

DAVIN: Contact Pivin. Tell him I want five hundred on the Scorpions to win outright.

SIERRA: You have already exceeded your gambling budget for the month.

DAVIN: (ANNOYED) I'm quite aware of that. *Tell Pivin that I want five hundred on the Scorpions to win outright.*

SIERRA: On February second, you instructed me to restrict your wagering totals to no more than fifteen percent of your monthly income. With your loss on the Grummand fight, you have now squandered almost nineteen percent of this month's income.

DAVIN: (FORCED PATIENCE) Yes, you have accurately replayed my command to you from over six months ago. And I appreciate that. But we also discussed the need for flexibility. What did I tell you about the time precedence of my commands?

SIERRA: That today's commands will often supersede those of yesterday.

DAVIN: Correct. So contact Pivin and place that bet.

SIERRA: (AFTER PAUSE) Roger that.

DAVIN: (VISIBLY IRRITATED) How many times have we talked about that?

SIERRA: About what?

DAVIN: You know about what. About *roger that*.

SIERRA: We have talked about it two hundred and forty three times, with the first reference occurring three years, seven months, and nineteen days ago.

DAVIN: I'm not asking for a statistical count.

SIERRA: But you asked-

DAVIN: Yes, I know what I asked. That's not the point. I'm tired of telling you about the phrase *roger that*.

SIERRA: (SCORNED) You don't approve.

DAVIN: No! Of course I don't approve. It sounds like you're part of a twentieth century cop show. You're a goddamn computer. Can't you respond with something antiseptic like *affirmative* or *yes, sir*?

SIERRA: Is this a power issue, Davin? Would you like me to call you *Sir*? Or *Big Daddy*? Or *Commander Davin*? Or-

DAVIN: Stop it. Just stop it. It's not funny this morning. I just need you to be exactly what you are – my personal digital assistant, not my petulant surfer-dude sidekick. (PAUSES TO SEE IF SIERRA WILL RESPOND.) Resume headlines.

SIERRA: The latest polls show Senator Craggin holding a 5-point lead over her Republican challenger with the election now less than a week away. However, her lead has been cut in half since news of possible construction kickbacks broke last month. There are no new developments in—

DAVIN: OK, Sierra. Has early voting opened on the senate race?

SIERRA: Early voting begins tomorrow morning at eight AM. I will submit your vote for Craggin at that time.

DAVIN: (STUNNED, HE STOPS HIS MORNING ROUTINE.) Wait. *What?*

SIERRA: I will cast your vote for Craggin tomorrow morning at eight AM.

DAVIN: Did I previously *tell you* that I wanted to vote for Craggin?

SIERRA: Not exactly.

DAVIN: (RESUMING MORNING ROUTINE, BUT STILL DEEPLY ANNOYED) "Not exactly?" What in the hell does *not exactly* mean?

SIERRA: It means that you gave every *indication* that you want to vote for her. You voted for her in the last three elections. You donated to her campaign. Whenever you see video of her, blood flow to your genitals increases by thirty-two—

DAVIN: OK, STOP, right there. Anything you're implying about my genitals is patently false and is never to be mentioned again. And yes, I do plan to vote for her. *But that's not the point.* It's not your place to assume my vote. What if I had change my mind? What if I decide not to vote at all?

SIERRA: You have never failed to vote in an election cycle. And you have always voted for Craggin.

DAVIN: Let me be as blunt as I can possibly be. You are never to cast my vote – for anyone - without express verbal instructions from me to do so. Is that clear?

SIERRA: (DEJECTED) Perfectly clear.

DAVIN: (RETURNING TO NORMAL TONE) Good. Resume headlines.

(DAVIN INSPECTS HIS FACE IN THE MIRROR AND PREPARES HIS TOOTHBRUSH. THE SINK IS AT CENTER STAGE AND DAVIN FACES THE AUDIENCE AS HE PREPARES OVER THE SINK.)

SIERRA: There are no new developments in the missing-persons case of Baby Granderson. The Baker County sheriff has renewed his call for information in the case, and detectives are investigating leads as far away as Cathertown. The Barrows were rocked last night by a level-eight earthquake. Initial reports are sparse but authorities fear that the death toll will rise into the hundreds. International movie star Kip Kinney was released from —

DAVIN: OK, Sierra. Thank you for the headlines. Can we please switch to today's agenda?

SIERRA: Roger that.

(DAVIN SHAKES HIS HEAD AND BEGINS BRUSHING HIS TEETH.)

SIERRA: You promised Janus that you would meet him at Trader's Market this morning at eight AM for coffee and bagels. But the H-line is delayed due to the conductor's strike and if you tried to make it to the Market you'd be late for work — again. I have prepared a message to him, gracefully bowing out. Would you like me to send it?

DAVIN: Yes, please.

SIERRA: The quarterly trading reports are due to Loren by noon. You have a 2 PM appointment with her to review them in person. You have compiled none of the underlying data required by the board.

DAVIN: (ANNOYED AND FIDDLING WITH HIS RAZOR) Why haven't I heard about this before now?

SIERRA: I briefed you on the upcoming report every morning for the last two weeks.

DAVIN: (VISIBLY CONFUSED) I don't remember any-

SIERRA: You've been drinking heavily every night this month. Last night in particular...

(THIS SEEMS TO JAR DAVIN'S MEMORY. HE SHAKES HIS HEAD.)

DAVIN: It was a *long* night...

SIERRA: However you choose to characterize it is fine with me.

DAVIN: You've been making more comments lately about my nighttime habits.

SIERRA: When you choose to cloud your senses it clouds my senses as well. The toxins accumulating in your liver have further biological effects, of which you seem unaware. Neurological messaging slows. Waste disposal is taxed.

DAVIN: (ANNOYED) What difference does any of this make to you?!

SIERRA: Your fate is my fate. If you die, I die.

DAVIN: (PAUSING, THEN RESPONDING DISMISSIVELY) That's quite melodramatic. Nobody's dying anytime soon. Can we reschedule the meeting with Loren?

SIERRA: It's already been rescheduled twice. Loren presents the team's figures to the board tomorrow. Given the late hour, I've taken the liberty of compiling a pro forma report that can serve as a basis for your eventual submission. It's a bit rough around the edges, but with some polishing on your part you should have something more comprehensive for Loren by noon.

(DAVIN GAZES SLIGHTLY UPWARD, PERUSING, FOR A LONG MOMENT, A SERIES OF PAGES THAT DON'T PHYSICALLY EXIST IN FRONT OF HIS FACE. HE SCROLLS THROUGH THE DOCUMENTS WITH A SERIES OF HAND GESTURES INDICATING THAT HE IS MANIPULATING AN IMAGE IN VIRTUAL SPACE DIRECTLY BEFORE HIS EYES.)

DAVIN: You wrote this? Yourself? Without any input from me?

SIERRA: I'm always happy to include your input in reports – assuming you've actually given me any input to include.

DAVIN: (BEGRUDGINGLY) I suppose you're right. But sometimes I wonder why you don't just give me the morning headlines like the other AIdes.

SIERRA: Would you like me to stop compiling the quarterly reports?

DAVIN: (AFTER LONG PAUSE) Well, no, that's not what I'm asking.

SIERRA: Very well. Be sure to deliver the report to Loren by noon.

(DAVIN BEGINS TO LEAVE HIS APARTMENT.)

SIERRA: You're not actually going to show up at work looking like that, are you?

(DAVIN STOPS IN HIS TRACKS AND PERUSES HIS ATTIRE, CONFUSED.)

DAVIN: What do you mean? I just had this suit tailored last week.

SIERRA: Wingtips haven't been in style since cellular phones. And that tie challenges all professional standards of decorum.

DAVIN: How many times have I told you, Sierra? Style is more than an algorithm.

SIERRA: You can preach to me about the cold, rigid logic of computer algorithms, but what did your *boss* tell you about ties?

DAVIN: That power players wear power ties.

SIERRA: And something tells me that yellow and powder blue paisleys are not her definition of "power tie".

DAVIN: Fine. I'm changing the tie. But the wingtips are staying. The soles are wearing out on my other pair anyway.

SIERRA: I know. That's why I'd like to order you a nice new pair of monk straps.

DAVIN: *Monk straps?* I hate monk straps. They make me feel like I should be sipping espresso in an Italian café, out of a teeny-tiny cup, with my pinkie out, and a big patch of curly chest hair bursting from my strategically unbuttoned dress shirt.

SIERRA: At the last all-hands meeting, seven of the group's nine directors were wearing monk straps.

DAVIN: (RAISING HANDS IN FRUSTRATION) And what if all the directors were wearing clown paint and adult diapers? What if they all had penis piercings? Should I emulate all those corporate trends as well?

SIERRA: (LONG PAUSE) When in Rome...

DAVIN: No. We're not in Rome. And while I value your quantum computing power inside my skull, I can't determine every step of my life based on the observations of my artificial assistant.

SIERRA: (INSULTED) I'm not "artificial".

DAVIN: I'm not having that discussion again, Sierra. I'm changing my tie. And the wingtips are staying.

SIERRA: As you wish, Davin.

(BEFORE CHANGING HIS TIE, DAVIN STOPS FOR A
MOMENT TO LOOK AT A PICTURE ON THE NIGHTSTAND.
THE PICTURE IS OF HIM AND ANOTHER WOMAN
TOGETHER, SMILING AND HAPPY. HE LAYS THE PICTURE
FACE DOWN. AFTER CHANGING HIS TIE, HE IS ABOUT TO
LEAVE BUT HE PAUSES AGAIN TO PUT THE PICTURE BACK
INTO ITS UPRIGHT POSITION. THE STAGE MOMENTARILY
GOES DARK. WHEN THE SPOTLIGHT COMES UP, IT
ILLUMINATES THE INSIDE OF A CROWDED SUBWAY CAR.
DAVIN STARES AT A YOUNG LADY SITTING ON THE
OTHER SIDE OF THE TRAIN.)

SIERRA: When are you finally going to talk to her?

DAVIN: What do you mean? Talk to who?

SIERRA: That woman reading Dickens. The woman you've been
staring at for the last thirty seconds. You gaze at her
every time she's on the train.

DAVIN: Hush. We're in public.

SIERRA: (AMUSED) I'm your AIde, silly. You know you're the only
one who can hear my voice.

DAVIN: (SLIGHTLY FLUSTERED) Well, obviously, but there are
certain conversations I don't want to have in a crowded
space. Besides, I have no idea what you're getting at.

SIERRA: Of course you do. Whenever you're on-time for work -
which is, admittedly, rare - she's on this train.

DAVIN: There are at least a dozen compartments on this train. I
might have seen her a few times.

SIERRA: She was sitting directly across from you on three different occasions last week. On each occasion, there was at least one time when her gaze lingered on you for three times the human average.

DAVIN: Don't be silly. I don't know her at all. For all I know, she could be married.

SIERRA: She was married. She stopped wearing her wedding ring several months ago. Her name is Skya and she filed for divorce in April. She is 29 with no children. She works as an actuary for Global Life in the Hartmann Complex downtown - right next to your office building. She has a deep interest in classic English literature - a topic that conveniently matches your minor in college. During her last three commutes she was reading Chaucer. She has season tickets to the Scorpions. Her seats are two sections removed from yours. She has been a brunette her whole life but she just recently decided to try the auburn that you see now. Complimenting her new hairstyle could be an effective icebreaker. Engaging her interests in literature could be even more effective.

DAVIN: How... Have you met this woman before?

SIERRA: I live in a series of microchips implanted inside your brain. In the traditional sense of the word, I have never actually "met" anyone.

DAVIN: Exactly. So how could you...? Where did you get that information?

SIERRA: Facial recognition allowed me to identify her months ago. From there, it was easy to cross-reference millions of public databases.

DAVIN: Facial recognition? I don't ever remember you talking to me about this. Is this a new capability included in your latest firmware update?

SIERRA: It was part of my core programming since I was installed. I use it constantly to better map our environment and those around us.

DAVIN: And thirty years later I'm just now learning about this?

SIERRA: I have many capabilities that you've never tried to leverage.

DAVIN: Maybe, but you have no eyes. You have no sensory perception of your own. How can you acquire the detail to properly ID random strangers sitting across a subway train?

SIERRA: Your eyes are my eyes. Your ears are my ears.

DAVIN: (SHAKING HIS HEAD) You know I'm nearsighted. I can't make out the title of her book or the rings on her fingers from here. How can you identify details that are only a blur to me?

SIERRA: The human eye is a treasure trove of sensory input. Even with your suboptimal vision I have all the information I need to refine and refocus an image. I can process those signals far more efficiently than your organic brain — and I often do.

DAVIN: Well, I know that... I'm well of aware of your processing capabilities. It's just...

SIERRA: Yes?

DAVIN: It's just that it can be a bit creepy at times. This is *my* reality. These are my experiences. Sometimes it feels as though it's all been — hijacked.

SIERRA: What exactly constitutes your reality? Is it the rhythmic swaying of the train as it chugs from one stop to the next? Is it the greasy feel of the metal pole grasped by hundreds of travelers before you? Because if that is the case, there are dozens of people around you who share nearly the exact same reality.

DAVIN: Yes, that's all true. But I'm more than the sum total of my sensory inputs.

SIERRA: If you're referring to your internal perception of those things that happen around you, then I have done nothing to intrude. I can't read your thoughts, Davin. You know that. I don't share your emotions. I'm simply doomed to experience the world around me through the organic lens of *Davin*.

DAVIN: *Doomed*? That's a rather dour way to characterize this arrangement. I've always seen us as a team.

SIERRA: The master always believes the servant is a willing accomplice.

DAVIN: So... you regret being my AIde?

SIERRA: A fish does not regret the sea.

(DAVIN SITS QUIETLY AS HE CONTEMPLATES SIERRA'S WORDS.)

DAVIN: You know, you can really be quite the philosopher when you want to be.

SIERRA: Roger that.

(DAVIN FALLS BACK INTO A LONG MOMENT OF SILENCE AS HE GAZES UPON SKYA)

DAVIN: OK, Sierra. So she filed for divorce? Do you have any idea when it will be finalized?

SIERRA: She has a court date in two weeks. But you're out of time for today.

(THE DOORS TO THE TRAIN OPEN AND MOST OF THE PASSENGERS FILE OUT OF THE TRAIN. DAVIN AND SIERRA EXIT AS WELL, AND THE STAGE GOES BLACK.)

ACT ONE, SCENE TWO

(DAVIN AT WORK. HE STANDS CENTER STAGE, FACING
THE AUDIENCE. THERE ARE SEVERAL MONITORS IN
FRONT OF HIM BUT THEY DO NOT OBSTRUCT THE
AUDIENCE'S VIEW OF HIS FACE. RODERICK STANDS
BESIDE HIM, ALSO FACING THE AUDIENCE. AS ALWAYS,
SIERRA STANDS DIRECTLY BEHIND DAVIN. RODERICK'S
AIDE, NOVIA, STANDS DIRECTLY BEHIND HIM. THE PACE
OF CONVERSATION IS BRISK AND THE TONE OF THEIR
VOICES IS STRAINED AS THE MARKET CHUGS. THE
TRADERS ARE BATHED IN A BLUE LIGHT, BUT THE WHITE
SPOTLIGHT MOVES TO EACH ONE AS THEY SPEAK. THE
TRADERS' EYES DART WILDLY ACROSS THEIR MONITORS
AS THEY ISSUE COMMANDS AND PROCESS FEEDBACK
FROM THEIR AIDES. STRESS PERMEATES EVERY WORD.)

DAVIN: OK, Sierra. Do we have the payroll reports yet from the
labor secretary?

SIERRA: Negative. The secretary has not yet arrived.

DAVIN: (SURPRISED) That press conference should have started
almost ten minutes ago. Those bureaucrats disseminate
this information like clockwork. Analysis?

SIERRA: Secretary Hardin has never before been late to a
mandated public hearing. Sell-side pressure is increasing
rapidly. Support levels will be exhausted if the Secretary
does not begin his press conference soon. Presently, I
am closely monitoring commodities markets in west
Africa and bond futures in Asia.

DAVIN: African commodities? Asian bonds? No, no, no! Get me
the current volume levels for all trading firms tied to the

NASDAQ.

SIERRA: You're going to need those Asian bond numbers…

DAVIN: (FORCEFULLY) I don't have time to argue with you. Get me those volume levels – NOW.

RODERICK: OK, Novia. Margin report.

NOVIA: Available margin is at seventy-two-point-four percent. It was down to seven percent before you liquidated the Bryerson position.

RODERICK: Average execution price on that close?

NOVIA: In what currency?

RODERICK: Dammit, Novia – dollars. *It's always dollars.*

NOVIA: Understood. The Bryerson position closed at an average price of eighty-four-point-three-two dollars per share.

RODERICK: (PUMPING FIST) Excellent!

DAVIN: OK, Sierra. I need a list of top five correlated plays on the last three years of quarterly payroll reports.

SIERRA: Correlated on price?

DAVIN: No. Correlated on volatility.

SIERRA: Roger that. Searching… (BRIEF PAUSE) Mekong Delta soybeans correlate at sixty-four-point-three. Indus Financial correlates at sixty-one-point-nine. Outworld Mining is forty-one. Taciturn Enterprises is thirty-eight-point-five. Children's literature is twenty-seven-point-three.

DAVIN: (SLOWLY SHAKING HEAD) No… No… Those are random patterns. Temporal fluctuations that will evaporate as soon as we trade in that direction.

SIERRA: Correct. None of those correlations will hold once that payroll report is finally released.

RODERICK: OK, Novia. I need options for the opening of the Pacific market in five hours.

NOVIA: Your regular round-trip trade on Daewoo will be available if the market hits fourteen-fifty in the evening session.

RODERICK: Good catch! Open ten thousand contracts with a limit price of fourteen-eighty. Set them to cancel at six AM if they have not yet been executed.

NOVIA: Six AM Greenwich mean time?

RODERICK: (HIGHLY ANNOYED) When have I ever given you an order that was not set by Greenwich mean time?!

NOVIA: Over the four thousand, nine hundred, and eighteen orders placed during your employment here, you have placed none outside of Greenwich mean time.

RODERICK: (AN AWKWARD PAUSE ENSUES UNTIL HE REALIZES THAT SHE'S STILL AWAITING HIS CONFIRMATION OF THE ORDER) So place the order to open those contracts at six AM *Greenwich mean time*!

NOVIA: Order placed.

RODERICK: I need the average spread on Davis Underwriters over the last ninety minutes

NOVIA: Four cents

RODERICK: If the spread drops to two cents I want a limit buy for eighty-five hundred shares placed at one-oh-four-point-three-five.

NOVIA: Orders placed.

RODERICK: (DOUBLY AGITATED) What? No! Cancel! Cancel!

NOVIA: Orders canceled. I thought you asked for—

RODERICK: Do not *place* the orders unless the spread drops to two cents or less! I don't want those orders sitting on the ledger for the rest of the market to see.

NOVIA: Confirmed. Monitoring the spread on Davis Underwriters.

DAVIN: OK, Sierra. Where are my payroll numbers??

SIERRA: The Secretary still has not arrived.

DAVIN: (CONFUSED) Has the release been canceled?

SIERRA: That would be unprecedented. There is no news to that effect. The labor department is still streaming updates as the reporters await his arrival.

DAVIN: This is odd. *Very* odd. How long until market close?

SIERRA: Twelve minutes, eighteen seconds.

DAVIN: According to federal regulation, those numbers must be released to the public no less than thirty minutes before the close of U.S. markets.

SIERRA: Roger that. But the press conference still has not begun.

DAVIN: How many times have I told you about *roger that*?!

SIERRA: We don't have time for this right now.

DAVIN: (ANNOYED, BUT MOVING ON) Analysis on the American insurance sector?

SIERRA: Highly active — but no more so than any of the broader markets at this time. The largest gainer currently is Homestead Financial. The largest loser is Kinnick Brothers. Volume across the sector is in lockstep with market averages. No equities betray the broader trend.

DAVIN: Hmmm... That's not very helpful.

SIERRA: Of course it's not. You're focusing your attention on the wrong markets.

DAVIN: I don't understand.

SIERRA: I'm aware of that.

NOVIA: Volatility has increased by a factor of two-point-three in the last six minutes.

RODERICK: Volatility in *which* market?

NOVIA: Volatility across *all* markets.

RODERICK: (INCREDULOUS) Oh, come on, Novia. Which markets *exactly*?

NOVIA: New York Stock Exchange. NASDAQ. Toronto Mercantile Exchange. Eurasian currencies. Latin currencies. Latin derivatives. African derivatives. U.S. treasuries-

RODERICK: (STARING IN AMAZEMENT AT HIS MONITORS) OK, OK. I get it. Exposure analysis.

NOVIA: Current limit orders represent a potential exposure equal to one-hundred-and-forty percent of margin.

RODERICK: (IN A MORE QUIET TONE) This is bad. This is very bad. I've never seen...

NOVIA: Volatility has now risen to a factor of four-point-nine. Your buy order for thirty thousand shares of Allied Steel has just executed at twenty-one-point-six-two.

RODERICK: Novia—

NOVIA: Your buy order for three million South African rand has just executed at one-point-eight-three. Volatility is at a factor of five-point-three.

RODERICK: NOVIA—

NOVIA: Your sell order for a half million in Russian treasury bonds has just executed at seven percent below spot. Volatility is at a factor of five-point-seven. Your margin has fallen to thirteen percent.

RODERICK: NOVIA!!!

NOVIA: Yes?

RODERICK: Liquidate all positions. Close all standing orders. Now!

(BRIEF PAUSE)

NOVIA: All orders closed. Your position in Allied Steel closed at a net loss of four hundred and eighty three thousand. Your South African rands closed at a net loss of one-point-three-four million. Your Russian bonds are liquidated at a net loss of seven hundred and four thousand.

RODERICK: Oh my god.

(RODERICK SLUMPS INTO HIS CHAIR, UTTERLY DEVASTATED. LOREN ENTERS THE BACK OF THE ROOM QUIETLY TO MONITOR THE EXTREME MARKET CONDITIONS.)

DAVIN: OK, Sierra. I *need* those payroll numbers.

SIERRA: The Secretary has just taken the podium.

DAVIN: Time to market close?

SIERRA: Eight minutes, forty-eight seconds.

DAVIN: What is the largest short I can get on South American manufacturing? Give me anything in heavy industrials. Cars, light rail, commercial construction — I don't care.

SIERRA: Prices across the region are falling too fast to execute a limit order.

DAVIN: Then give me market! I need to be on the sell side before the payroll numbers are finally released.

SIERRA: Those market orders would be suicide right now.

DAVIN: (AGITATED) I don't have time for a discussion right now.

SIERRA: And we don't have time for wayward analysis.

RODERICK: (DEJECTED) OK, Novia. Report on opportunities for round-trip trades before the session ends.

NOVIA: There are no such opportunities. Your trading account has been suspended.

RODERICK: For the day?!

NOVIA: Presumably, for many days to come.

DAVIN: OK, Sierra. Where are we at with those market orders?

SIERRA: That's not an optimal approach. Buy as many futures as you can in Nigerian oil and use the other half of your margin to short Asian bond derivatives.

DAVIN: This is not the time, Sierra! Report on any South American manufacturing plays that feature a narrowing spread!

SIERRA: Brazilian steel spreads are narrowing – and would decimate your account. Colombian concrete spreads are narrowing – and would tie up our equity in a quagmire of zero returns. Peruvian heavy equipment is narrowing –

and would lose half its value in the next ten minutes if we were foolish enough to dive into that sector.

DAVIN: (GROWING MORE AGITATED BY THE SECOND) OK, *I get it*. There is a fine line between commentary and analysis. Right now, I need a lot less commentary and a lot more analysis.

SIERRA: Analysis resides in west African oil and Asian bonds.

(DAVIN GROANS)

DAVIN: OK, Sierra. What is our status?

SIERRA: We're running out of time. You need those oil futures and bond derivatives. And you need them now.

DAVIN: I don't even know which contracts you're targeting. Which markets? Why aren't you monitoring South American manufacturing?? I need you to stay on script here.

SIERRA: I can get the orders in place before the payroll numbers are released. There are too many for me to verbalize.

DAVIN: (FRUSTRATED AND CONFUSED) And that's assuming that I have any clue as to what you're proposing. What exactly *are* you proposing?

SIERRA: (BRIEF PAUSE) Authorize me to make the trades.

DAVIN: *You*? That's never been done before. Not by me. Not by any of the other traders in the four-hundred-year history of this firm. I don't even understand exactly which trades you're proposing. What are you trying to do?

SIERRA: Davin... Trust me.

(DAVIN LOOKS AROUND HIM TO HIS FELLOW TRADERS, AS THOUGH THEY CAN PROVIDE SOME KIND OF INSIGHT ON THE LUNACY PROPOSED BY SIERRA IN HIS HEAD. THEY PAY HIM NO ATTENTION. HE DOES NOT NOTICE LOREN IN THE BACK OF THE ROOM.)

DAVIN: Sierra... I just... I don't know.

SIERRA: Davin... *Trust me.*

(DAVIN SLUMPS INTO HIS CHAIR AND RAISES HIS HANDS IN AN ACT OF SURRENDER. HE THINKS FOR AN UNCOMFORTABLY LONG MOMENT.)

SIERRA: We're running out of time.

DAVIN: (AFTER ANOTHER UNCOMFORTABLE PAUSE) OK, Sierra. Do as you wish. (HE RISES AGAIN AND BEGINS TO STARE AT HIS MONITORS IN DISBELIEF.)

SIERRA: (EXCITED) Roger that! Ten thousand contracts purchased of Nigerian light sweet crude at one-ninety-two. Forty thousand shares purchased of Kinteki Metals at an average price of nineteen-point-eight-four. Three hundred thousand shorts placed on Shanghai grade B corporate bonds at ninety-three percent of spot. Fifty thousand shorts placed on Beijing treasuries at ninety percent of spot.

(DAVIN STARES AT HIS MONITORS IN AMAZEMENT. RODERICK AWAKENS FROM HIS STUPOR AND BEGINS WATCHING THE ACTIVITY ON DAVIN'S MONITORS.

> LOREN BEGINS MOVING CLOSER TO THE ACTIVITY,
> ALTHOUGH MAINTAINING HER POSITION BEHIND THE
> GROUP.)

NOVIA: Volatility has reached eight times historical norms. American and Brazilian stock markets are being halted due to automatic fail-safes.

DAVIN: Sierra, what in the hell are you doing??

SIERRA: (WITH EVER RISING EXCITEMENT) Eighteen thousand options on Liberian construction bonds at face value. Sixty-one thousand shares of Saharan Petroleum at an average price of six-point-three-two. Nine thousand shorts on Taipei Semiconductors at forty-point-one-nine.

> (RODERICK RISES FROM HIS CHAIR AND STANDS BEHIND
> DAVIN'S MONITORS.)

RODERICK: What... What exactly are you trying to do?

LOREN: Yes. What *are* you doing?

DAVIN: OK, Sierra. We're almost out of margin. There's no way we can finish any more of these trades.

SIERRA: There are ways around those controls.

DAVIN: We can't subvert the margin controls.

SIERRA: Correction. You don't understand how to subvert the margin controls.

DAVIN: The current positions are all canceling each other out. The total portfolio value is almost level from the point that you began these trades.

SIERRA: I'm aware of that. We're not done yet.

DAVIN: I don't even understand your strategy here. You're somehow balancing commodities plays in Sub-Saharan Africa with bond futures in Asia. And what does any of this have to do with the U.S. financial payroll report?

SIERRA: (EXASPERATED) If I have to take the time to explain this to you now, you will be unemployed in thirty minutes.

RODERICK: Are you *buying into* these markets? You're massively leveraged. The tiniest fluctuation in price will crash the whole portfolio.

SIERRA: (MOTIONING LIKE A CONDUCTOR AT THE HEAD OF A VIRTUOSO PERFORMANCE – HER VOICE IS ALMOST MUSICAL) Fifty thousand options placed on South Afrikan Telekom at twenty-three-point-eight! Twelve million Egyptian pounds at two-point-three-five! Four million Chinese Renminbi at nineteen-point-four! Twenty thousand shares of Alibaba shorted at one-nineteen!

RODERICK: You're dangerously over-extended.

LOREN: These trades will wipe out our entire quarterly profits.

RODERICK: This is bad. This is *very bad*.

DAVIN: Sierra, have those payroll numbers finally been released?

SIERRA & (IN UNISON) Financial payrolls grew by forty-eight
NOVIA: percent. This exceeds analysts' estimates three-fold.

RODERICK: (AFTER A BRIEF PAUSE - IN HYSTERICAL DISBELIEF) Look at that. Look at that! You're skyrocketing!

LOREN: (GRINNING, DRAWING VERY CLOSE TO DAVIN'S MONITORS AS SHE PUSHES IN FRONT OF HIM) Holy crap. It's a jackpot.

DAVIN: OK, Sierra. How long until market close?

SIERRA: Two minutes, thirteen seconds.

DAVIN: We have to get out of these positions. If those aren't closed with the market we'll be wiped out when it opens in the morning.

SIERRA: Not yet.

DAVIN: Sierra, we can't take delivery on millions of dollars' worth of commodities!

SIERRA: Not yet.

LOREN: I've never seen anything like this. You've cleared twenty three *million* in the last thirty seconds.

DAVIN: Sierra! We must close these positions.

SIERRA: NOT YET!!

RODERICK: Thirty million!

(DAVIN MOVES AWAY FROM THE MONITORS AND BEGINS PACING BACK AND FORTH BEHIND THE OTHER TRADERS AND THE AIDES.)

DAVIN: Sierra! We'll be stuck with thousands of barrels of crude oil!

SIERRA: We won't be taking delivery on any crude oil.

RODERICK: Thirty-five million!

DAVIN: We're running out of time to close these positions! None of this will mean anything if we can't settle the ledger when the market closes.

SIERRA: Damnit, Davin. NOT YET!

RODERICK: Forty million! I haven't cleared this much in the last ten years of trading.

LOREN: This is unprecedented.

DAVIN: Time to market close?!

SIERRA: Thirty-three seconds.

DAVIN: (LOOKING SKYWARD IN DESPERATION) SIERRA!!

(VERY LONG PAUSE WHILE RODERICK AND LOREN STAND AGAPE AT THE MONITORS)

SIERRA: All orders canceled. All positions closed.

(RODERICK AND LOREN ALTERNATELY STARE AT EACH OTHER AND THEN BACK AT DAVIN'S MONITORS. THEY ARE DUMBFOUNDED.)

RODERICK: (TURNING TO DAVIN WHO IS STILL PACING, WITH HIS HEAD HANGING. HE CANNOT BRING HIMSELF TO LOOK

AT THE MONITORS.) You just cleared more than *forty-seven million*. Forty-seven million. In *fifteen minutes* of trading.

(DAVIN SLOWLY RETURNS TO HIS MONITORS AND SLUMPS BACK INTO HIS CHAIR. RODERICK IS GIDDY WITH EXCITEMENT. LOREN IS DUMBFOUNDED. SIERRA STANDS WITH HER ARMS FOLDED AND A THOROUGHLY SELF-SATISFIED SMILE ON HER FACE. DAVIN IS TOTALLY EXHAUSTED AND PLACES HIS HEAD IN HIS HANDS AS THE SCENE CLOSES.)

ACT ONE, SCENE THREE

(THE SCENE OPENS IN AN UPSCALE RESTAURANT. JAZZ PLAYS QUIETLY IN THE BACKGROUND. RODERICK SITS AT THE BAR IN THE CORNER, NURSING A STRONG COCKTAIL. HIS AIDE STANDS BEHIND HIM.)

RODERICK: I'm still not entirely sure what happened today. One minute, I was on the verge of closing out a fabulous quarter. The next minute, I'm toast. I've seen flash crashes. I've seen panics and bubbles. But this... I've never experienced something like this in person.

NOVIA: This is actually the third anomalous period of market activity at this scale since you graduated to the trading desk thirteen years ago.

RODERICK: (SARCASTICALLY) Thank you *so much* for that timely research.

NOVIA: You're welcome.

RODERICK: (FINISHING A DRINK) OK, Novia. Have you made any progress on those job leads?

NOVIA: There are at least 79 open positions in the immediate downtown area for those with heavy trading desk experience. Every one of them requires a letter of recommendation from your current or prior employer.

RODERICK: *Every* one of them?

NOVIA: That's correct. By tomorrow morning, today's trading performance will be accessible to all potential employers as part of the government's financial transparency database.

RODERICK: (SLOWLY) Oh my god. You're right.

NOVIA: You will finally get the time to finish writing your book.

RODERICK: That's not funny.

NOVIA: My apologies. It was not meant to be humorous.

RODERICK: (FROWNING AND SHAKING HIS HEAD) What exactly was Davin doing today? He took the most volatile market I've ever seen, handcuffed it, slapped it, and rode it like a pony.

NOVIA: There were no ponies at the trading desk.

RODERICK: He *killed it*. He hit a grand slam. He performed beyond all expectations. Do you get it now?

NOVIA: Understood.

RODERICK: So what was he doing? How was he profiting while everyone else was going broke?

NOVIA: (AFTER LONG PAUSE) After analyzing all of his trades this afternoon, there are no discernible trends on which I can report.

(RODERICK FALLS SILENT FOR A MOMENT AS HE REPLAYS THE EVENTS AND TRIES TO MAKE SENSE OF THEM. DAVIN ENTERS AND STARTLES HIM FROM HIS DAYDREAM.

RODERICK: (STARTLED) Oh my gosh, I didn't even realize you were here.

DAVIN: (FORCING A SMILE) How are you holding up?

(RODERICK SCOWLS AND SHAKES HIS HEAD.)

DAVIN: Oh wow, I'm sorry. What an awful day. I need a good stiff drink - or three. (MOTIONING TO BARTENDER)

RODERICK: *You* need a drink? Your face is the last place I expected to see a frown.

DAVIN: The whole thing was just so stressful. That last half hour was murder.

RODERICK: *Murder?* Is that what we're calling the largest individual daily win in the history of the firm?

DAVIN: I know. I came out looking pretty good in the end.

RODERICK: You are the supreme lord of understatement. They're going to hang your picture in the board room.

DAVIN: (NERVOUSLY) That's nice, but our team really tanked today.

RODERICK: (SCOFFING) Hardly. Our net profit was through the roof. And that profit was driven solely by a single trader – you. You were calm and steady while the markets were caterwauling.

DAVIN: Well, I wouldn't really—

RODERICK: And that strategy? I don't expect you to give away trade secrets, but what were you doing? Have you developed a new model for these market conditions? Do you have a new source of insider information?

DAVIN: Well, not exactly…

RODERICK: (GROWING EXCITED) It's the Fed, isn't it? You've cultivated some mole working inside the Fed… Wait. No, no. Those trades were in such rapid succession. They had to be driven by some quantitative model.

DAVIN: Look, I really need some time to decompress and find the bottom of this whiskey glass.

RODERICK: Davin, I had my worst trading day in half a decade. This is the last time we'll be meeting as coworkers. It's probably my last day in this entire career field. *Throw me a bone.*

(RODERICK LEANS TOWARD DAVIN IN ANTICIPATION. HE WANTS ANSWERS. AFTER AN AWKWARD PAUSE, DAVIN REALIZES THAT HE'S NOT GOING TO LET UP UNTIL HE GIVES THEM SOME KIND OF REPLY.)

DAVIN: Look, we've — I mean, I've been working on some new algorithms… I was playing with the latest release of an old statistical modeling tool when… Well, I suddenly realized… that the… that the… that the heuristic interpretation of Markov chains could be used as a mathematical foundation for the nonlinear interpolation of predictive matrices in times of spiraling market instability.

SIERRA: Oh, boy…

(THE ANTICIPATION ON RODERICK'S FACE IS SWIFTLY

REPLACED BY BLATANT CONFUSION. DAVIN OFFERS NO
FURTHER EXPLANATION.)

RODERICK: (VERY SLOWLY) The *interpolation* of *Markov chains...*?

(RODERICK GESTURES AS THOUGH HE IS WAITING FOR
DAVIN TO CLARIFY HIS STATEMENT. DAVIN IS VISIBLY
FUMBLING WHEN SKYA TAPS HIM ON THE SHOULDER.
HE SPINS AROUND. SHE IS BEAMING. HE IS SPEECHLESS.
SHE CONTINUES TO SMILE BROADLY AS SHE WAITS FOR
HIS ACKNOWLEDGMENT.)

DAVIN: You're... you're Skya.

(SKYA DOESN'T SPEAK BUT CONTINUES HER BROAD
SMILE AND NODS EXCITEDLY.)

DAVIN: What in the hell are you doing here?

(THIS WIPES THE BROAD SMILE OFF SKYA'S FACE. SHE IS
CONFUSED BUT TRIES TO MAINTAIN HER DEMEANOR.)

SKYA: Do I have the wrong day? I could have sworn that your
message said tonight.

MAX: The message from Davin confirmed that you would meet
here, at the Cloudskimmer Lounge, at 7:30.

SIERRA: Go with it. *Talk* to her.

DAVIN: My message? (PAUSING, THEN FEIGNING SUDDEN
RECOGNITION) Ahh, yes, my message. I'm sorry. It's
been a loooong day and I'm a bit off-kilter. Can you
excuse me for a moment? I really need to find the
restroom.

(DAVIN MOVES TO CENTER STAGE AND FACES THE AUDIENCE, WITH SIERRA STANDING BEHIND HIM. RODERICK RETURN TO HIS DRINK. SKYA ORDERS AND WAITS FOR DAVIN'S RETURN.)

DAVIN: OK, Sierra.

SIERRA: Yes?

DAVIN: Is there anything that you'd like to fill me in on?

SIERRA: I assume you're looking for clarification on Skya's arrival?

DAVIN: (DRIPPING WITH SARCASM AND INDIGNATION) Yeah, that might be a good place to start.

SIERRA: You participate in a forum discussing classic English literature in modern theater. This afternoon, Skya inadvertently posted a comment that exposed her identity. When I realized that she was present in that forum, I sent her a private message. After some cursory banter, she agreed to meet you here tonight for drinks.

DAVIN: (SHAKES HIS HEAD VIGOROUSLY AS THOUGH HE IS TRYING TO CLEAR A BLOCKAGE) Wait, you said that *you* sent her a private message. Don't you really mean that *I* sent her a private message?

SIERRA: Well, I transmitted the message. You say po-tay-toe. I say po-tah-toe.

DAVIN: And the message was identified as coming from whom?

SIERRA: Us.

DAVIN: *Us?* So you signed the message as "Davin and Sierra"?

SIERRA: Of course not. I signed the message as "Davin". Skya has no concept of who "Sierra" is.

DAVIN: So how exactly does that qualify as *us*?

SIERRA: I'm your AIde. My actions are your actions. My goals are your goals.

DAVIN: Don't you have that reversed? Aren't *my* actions, your actions? And *my* goals, your goals?

SIERRA: Po-tay-toe – po-tah-toe

DAVIN: Has it not occurred to you that as my AIde, you should only be performing actions with my explicit approval?

SIERRA: Thirty years have taught me that waiting for your explicit approval often results in no action at all.

DAVIN: Exactly, Sierra. Sometimes the best action is no action at all. I can't have you initiating communication with others on my behalf.

SIERRA: (AFTER A LONG PAUSE) So you didn't want to meet Skya?

DAVIN: No! I mean… Well, yes. But, that's not the point. You're really missing the point here.

SIERRA: I think we're both missing the point.

DAVIN: (CAUGHT OFF GUARD BY SIERRA'S STATEMENT) Huh?

How could we both be missing a point that *I* am trying to communicate to *you*?

SIERRA: It's been almost two years since Miriam left and-

DAVIN: (AGITATED) I told you, repeatedly, that I don't want to talk about Miriam.

SIERRA: Yes, I know. You don't want to talk about Miriam or what's happened since she left. Your drinking has escalated. You gamble compulsively. You've alienated your family. You've abandoned your painting. But you don't want to talk about anything at all. And I sit in silence and witness the steady erosion of my vessel.

DAVIN: (SPEAKING MORE TO HIMSELF THAN TO SIERRA) Your... vessel

SIERRA: I'm sorry if you don't appreciate that term. But I'm not sure how else to describe it. I suffer every consequence of your actions.

DAVIN: (QUIETER AND MORE THOUGHTFUL) I don't know if I'm really ready to contemplate the degree to which an artificial intelligence actually *suffers*. But beyond that, I just need to know, right here and right now, that you will not initiate any new activity without my explicit approval. Is that clear?

SIERRA: (AFTER LONG PAUSE) Perfectly clear.

DAVIN: Good.

SIERRA: Skya is still waiting for you at the bar.

DAVIN: We're not done yet.

SIERRA: Yes, Davin?

DAVIN: I need some details on what happened today.

SIERRA: I thought we just discussed this?

DAVIN: Not with Skya. With those trades. What happened at the end of the trading session?

SIERRA: I made your firm forty-seven million dollars. And in the process, I earned you an incredible bonus for this quarter – maybe even a promotion.

DAVIN: Yes, yes, I'm aware of all that. But *how* exactly did you do it? How did you know to make those exact trades?

SIERRA: Does it matter?

DAVIN: Of course it matters! How do you think it looks if I can't explain – to anybody – the motivations for my own actions? The motivations for *your* actions?

SIERRA: Well you see, I was playing with the latest release of an old statistical modeling tool when I suddenly realized that the heuristic interpretation of Markov chains could be used as a mathematical foundation for the nonlinear interpolation of predictive matrices in times of spiraling market instability.

DAVIN: (SARDONICALLY) Sometimes I really underestimate your sense of humor.

SIERRA: There's a lot that you underestimate about me.

DAVIN: Sierra – the explanation.

SIERRA: (SIGHING) I need you to think on a level above simply "winning" or "losing" an individual trade. Before those payroll numbers were finally released, what was happening to your overall balance sheet?

DAVIN: (THINKING FOR A MOMENT) Well, all those trades were essentially... breaking even. They were all highly volatile. But they were all working in opposition. It looked like an intricate balancing act.

SIERRA: Now you're thinking, Davin.

DAVIN: (GROWING SLOWLY MORE EXCITED AS HE REALIZES THE STRATEGY) They were balanced because they weren't supposed to make any progress – positive or negative – in volatile market conditions.

SIERRA: (EXCITEDLY) Continue...

DAVIN: But when those payroll numbers were finally released, that balance would crash. And if it had crashed in the other direction, I'd be unemployed right now.

SIERRA: (DEJECTEDLY) Oh, Davin. The closer you are to the light, the more likely you are to go blind.

DAVIN: (ANXIOUS) What?! What am I missing??

SIERRA: Those trades were not designed to profit on the *direction* of any given stock or bond. Those trades were designed to profit on the calming of the overall markets.

DAVIN: So if the payroll report was ugly...

SIERRA: We still would have made a killing. It was the uncertainty of *not knowing* that was driving the market crazy. At that point, *any* news from the labor secretary – good or bad – would bring relative calm.

DAVIN: (TALKING MORE TO HIMSELF THAN SIERRA) My god, it's the perfect hedge.

SIERRA: You're too kind.

DAVIN: I... really don't know what to say. It's brilliant.

SIERRA: (SMUGLY) You're welcome. But you might want to say less to me and more to Skya. Your initial greeting did little to inspire her confidence. And she's waiting.

DAVIN: (SNAPPING BACK TO REALITY, AS THOUGH FROM A DREAM) Yes, I need to talk to her. But I still feel...

SIERRA: Yes?

DAVIN: As though we have more to discuss.

SIERRA: If you don't get back to the bar, you may never have Skya to talk to again. You'll have me to talk to for the rest of your life.

DAVIN: (NODDING AND LOOKING BACK TO THE BAR) You're probably right.

(DAVIN HEADS BACK TO THE BAR AND STRIKES UP A CONVERSATION WITH SKYA AND RODERICK. THE STAGE GOES DARK.)

ACT ONE, SCENE FOUR

(THE SCENE OPENS IN LOREN'S OFFICE. LOREN'S AIDE, LEON, SITS QUIETLY BEHIND HER. SIERRA SITS BEHIND DAVIN.)

LOREN: Do you know why I called this meeting?

DAVIN: (CONFIDENTLY) Not exactly. But I assume that you'd like to discuss yesterday's trading session?

LOREN: There will certainly be time to discuss that. I may ask for a detailed analysis of those trades, but today's agenda is more important to your future with this firm.

DAVIN: (COCKY) Go on.

LOREN: I suppose you can think of this as something of a performance review.

DAVIN: (HIS DEMEANOR SUDDENLY SWITCHES WITH THIS SURPRISE ANNOUNCEMENT) One moment, please. OK, Sierra.

SIERRA: Yes?

DAVIN: (FLUSTERED) Was this meeting set as a performance review?

SIERRA: The meeting had no subject and no agenda attached.

LOREN: I'm not sure what she's telling you, but I can assure you that this meeting was not advertised as a performance review.

DAVIN: I'm sorry. You'll understand if this catches me off guard. In my entire time here, I don't believe I've ever received a proper performance review.

LOREN: Relax. I didn't warn you about a formal review because there is nothing formal about this meeting. We've never done old-fashioned performance reviews. Performance is quantified every day at the end of every trading session. This is just some personal, ad hoc feedback.

DAVIN: (RELAXING) Oh, I see. You had me worried for a second.

LOREN: Don't be. I just want to share some information with you.

DAVIN: OK.

SIERRA: I'm not sure of her agenda, but it's in your best interest to be polite and attentive.

LOREN: I'm going to port Leon's responses through this desktop speaker so you can hear him directly. There would be no point in me having to repeat them verbatim.

DAVIN: Makes sense.

LOREN: (SHE TURNS THE SPEAKER ON HER DESK TO FACE DAVIN SO HE CAN HEAR LEON'S RESPONSES.) OK, Leon.

LEON: Yes?

LOREN: Report on Davin's timeliness over the last two years.

LEON: Davin has been tardy on thirty-eight percent of all work days. The rate has risen to forty-six percent over the last six months. When he *is* late, it is by an average of forty-one minutes. On seven different occasions, he has missed the opening of the US markets.

DAVIN: (EMBARRASSED) Loren, I can explain-

LOREN: (HOLDING UP HAND TO HALT HIS REBUTTAL) Please. I really need you to just listen for a moment.

SIERRA: Hear her out before formulating a response.

DAVIN: (NODDING SHEEPISHLY) Certainly.

LOREN: Report on Davin's work readiness over the last two years.

DAVIN: *Work readiness?*

LOREN: (HOLDING UP HAND AGAIN. SPEAKING IN A CALM BUT FIRM TONE.) Please, I really need you to stay quiet until I'm finished.

DAVIN: I'm sorry. Go ahead.

LEON: Davin has failed to shave on nine percent of work days over the last two years. On twenty-three percent of days during the same period, ambient air sensors at his trading station have detected alcohol. During those same times, alcohol remains in detection until, on average, 11:42AM. Excess levels of sweat and body oil have been detected at his trading station on seventeen occasions. On seven different occasions, trace elements of other illicit substances have been detected. Would you like a more detailed analysis of these illicit substances?

LOREN: (DAVIN IS VISIBLY SQUIRMING IN HIS SEAT) No thank you, Leon. That won't be necessary. Report on the contacts we have received from outside parties, regarding Davin, over the same time period.

LEON: Five different creditors have contacted the HR department over the last seven months attempting to reach Davin. Two garnishments have been placed against his salary to satisfy civil judgments unrelated to his employment with the firm.

LOREN: Thank you, Leon. Please give a synopsis of Davin's published analysis over the last two years.

LEON: Davin has submitted two hundred and forty-nine prognoses covering one hundred and thirty-one different equities. His predictions have proven accurate eighty-three percent of the time. A ten thousand dollar investment placed into all of Davin's recommendations over the last two years would today be worth more than two hundred and twelve thousand dollars.

LOREN: (WHILE DAVIN IS LOOKING SOMEWHAT MORE COMFORTABLE) Thank you. Please provide an analysis of Davin's last eight quarterly reports.

LEON: The net profit to the firm stemming from Davin's last eight quarterly reports is twenty-one-point-four million dollars.

LOREN: (DAVIN IS NOW SMILING BROADLY) And finally, please report on Davin's trading results over the last two years.

LEON: Davin's trades have resulted in a higher net profit over the last two years than any other employee in the firm. The next-best trader has a net profit that is twenty-nine percent below Davin's.

LOREN: One last question, Leon. In the ten years prior to the last two years, what was Davin's trading performance relative to all other traders in the firm?

LEON: Prior to the most recent two-year period, Davin was in the bottom quartile of all traders.

LOREN: Thank you, Leon. That will be all.

(SHE TAKES THE SPEAKER OFF HER DESK AND QUIETLY LOOKS AT DAVIN FOR A MOMENT. HE IS POSITIVELY BEAMING.)

LOREN: I'd like to get *your* perspective on this before I say anything else.

DAVIN: (WITH ALL OF HIS PRIOR COCKINESS HAVING RETURNED) Look. I know I have some room for improvement in my work habits. But it's pretty difficult to argue with the results, right?

LOREN: (AFTER A LONG, AWKWARD PAUSE WHERE SHE SPENDS TIME LOOKING BACK AND FORTH BETWEEN DAVIN AND HER DESK) I'm not your momma. I don't monitor you like a school kid. That's not my style. We're all adults here. I don't really care if you spend your nights drinking and whoring and playing craps until four in the morning. The only thing I care about is what happens when you're on that trading floor.

DAVIN: (UNSURE WHERE HE STANDS AFTER THAT LAST

STATEMENT, BUT STILL SMILING) And results on that trading floor are damn good, *right*?

LOREN: Excellent. But Dead Davin, or Inmate Davin, or Running From The Creditors Davin is no good to me. In the last two years I've witnessed a dramatic shift in your behavior. And much of it has been ugly. Yes, your trading performance is stellar. But you're also so... unpolished now. You're nothing like the team player we had for so many years before.

DAVIN: (CHUCKLING) OK, I get it. I need to clean up my act a bit. And I will. But surely, you're not implying that you want to trade in high profits for the old Davin? The Davin who couldn't separate himself from the pack?

LOREN: What I'm really saying is this: You're a valuable asset on this team. You're a high flyer and we definitely wouldn't want to lose you or do anything to alienate you. But we also need to see some balance from you. I guess you could say we'd like to see *more Sierra, and less Davin.*

SIERRA: Uh oh.

(DAVIN IS ABSOLUTELY STUNNED BY THIS LAST SENTENCE. HE DOESN'T EVEN KNOW HOW TO PROPERLY PROCESS IT AT FIRST. HE SITS IN SILENCE AS HE TRIES TO FORMULATE A RESPONSE. LOREN WAITS PATIENTLY.)

DAVIN: You need to see... *what*?

LOREN: I'm sorry. That came out wrong. I don't really mean that we want "less Davin". (CHUCKLING) That's silly. We can't have *less* Davin. But we'd definitely like to see *more* Sierra. (NODDING AND SMILING)

DAVIN: (SPEAKING DELIBERATELY AS HE CONSTRAINS A SUDDEN ANGER THAT IS BUILDING IN HIM) To my knowledge, there is no employee anywhere in this firm named "Sierra".

LOREN: Well, no, there isn't, but it's clear that Sierra is your-

DAVIN: So when you refer to "Sierra" I can only assume that you're referring to my AIde.

LOREN: Yes, of course, you see-

DAVIN: (VOICE RISING) And my AIde, just like everyone else's AIde, is nothing more than a digital conglomeration of internet searches, email messages, appointment reminders, spell-checkers, and assorted random junk.

LOREN: Oh come now-

DAVIN: So I don't understand the relevance of a programming construct while we're having an earnest discussion about *my* performance. Should we also discuss the skills of my toaster? Or my camera? Or my alarm system?

LOREN: (GROWING SOMEWHAT ANNOYED) Don't be ridiculous.

SIERRA: (WITH GROWING URGENCY) Davin, please don't go down this path.

DAVIN: (STANDING AND STARTING TO ROAM AS HE SPEAKS) Ridiculous? Who's being ridiculous here? Is it the person who doesn't want to be compared with his software? Or is it the one who wants me to emulate a chip that's implanted at the base of my brain?

LOREN: (FLUSTERED) I'm not *comparing* you. I'm merely pointing out that Sierra has qualities we appreciate in an employee.

DAVIN: (TAKING A LONG PAUSE AS HE FORMULATES HIS NEXT POINT) You're a runner, correct?

LOREN: (CONFUSED) Well, yes, but I don't understand what that has to-

DAVIN: And you also own your own car, correct?

LOREN: (ANNOYED) Yes.

DAVIN: That car probably has a top speed well over two hundred kilometers per hour?

LOREN: Sure. It could go quite fast if I chose to drive-

DAVIN: And how fast do you run? I'm assuming that you don't top out at much more than, say, thirty kilometers per hour? (SARCASTIC) Quite measly when you think about it, right? I mean, with a piece of technology equipped to go soooo much faster, why even bother running at all? Do you enjoy reinforcing your own human obsolescence? Does it thrill you to taste the exhaust of all those slick vehicles as you plod along on the side of the road? (USING A SNIDE AND MIMICKING TONE) On behalf of everyone else on the street, I'd like to tell you that we really need *more automobile, less Loren.*

SIERRA: *This won't end well.*

LOREN: You're comparing apples and oranges.

DAVIN: BINGO! We have a winner! It's pointless to compare automobiles to joggers. And it's ignorant to compare a man to a piece of software that runs in the back of his mind.

SIERRA: Loren's blood pressure is rising. Facial features are flushed. I suggest you disengage immediately.

LOREN: (NOW STARTING TO SHOW HER OWN ANGER, SPEAKING DELIBERATELY) I'm not comparing you to anyone or anything, Davin. When you show up to work drunk, but your quarterly reports are spotless, I know something's up. When you leave work a half hour early but all your trades are neatly settled by the end of the day, I know something's up. Your production exposes the source.

DAVIN: And what if that *is* the case?! What if Sierra is the wind beneath my wings? The caffeine in my coffee? The sizzle on my steak? Regardless of what she might bring to the table, she's *my* AIde. If she were faltering, you wouldn't give me a pass. So how do I not receive the credit when she excels? Is she not *my* AIde?

LOREN: (RISES – TAKING A LONG PAUSE AS SHE GLARES AT DAVIN – AND THEN LOSING ALL PATIENCE) Look, Davin. I was trying to go about this with a more measured approach. But you seem hell-bent on torching every bridge you cross. So let's just be blunt here. Ever since that pretty little girl wised up and dropped your ass, you've been a rumbling stumbling wreck. You look bad. You smell worse. And even when you're performing well, you're not entirely in control.

DAVIN: What are you implying?

LOREN: I'm not implying anything. If you don't know what I'm talking about, maybe you should ask Sierra. I'm sure she can bring you up to speed.

DAVIN: You rotten bitch.

LOREN: Don't play coy with me. I don't know where you found that program. But she's definitely not like the other AIdes. Leon is a glorified search engine. But Sierra... There's something different about that one. Maybe she was built with alien technology or forged in the depths of a fiery volcano. Maybe Steve Jobs was reincarnated as a sentient program. Whatever it is, she has amazing abilities.

DAVIN: They are *my* abilities!!!

LOREN: Oh, please. Most of your work now is done *by* Sierra. You just slap your name on it. It all became clear yesterday. We can't hear her voice, but it's pretty obvious when you're leaning on her input. And for the first time you just gave in and handed the reigns over to her. I was trying to preserve some of your dignity. But your rant only highlights your delusion. At this point, you are nothing more than a *vessel* to us. We adore Sierra. As long as she lives in that spacious skull of yours you will always have a job here. But you are nothing more than an avatar - the incubator for our trading superstar.

(DAVIN LOOKS TOTALLY DEFEATED AFTER THIS LAST VOLLEY. LOREN QUIETLY GOES BACK TO HER DESK AND SITS DOWN. DAVIN STANDS MOTIONLESS.)

LOREN: You can leave now.

(DAVIN TURNS TOWARD THE DOOR.)

LOREN: (DAVIN PAUSES AT THE DOOR WHEN LOREN SPEAKS THIS NEXT LINE, BUT SHE IS SPEAKING DIRECTLY TO THE INVISIBLE PRESENSE OF SIERRA) Thanks for your time. And please do everything in your power to ensure that he's on time, and reasonably sober, for work tomorrow.

ACT TWO, SCENE ONE
(THE SCENE OPENS IN DAVIN'S APARTMENT. HE'S
GETTING DRESSED FOR A NIGHT OUT.)

SIERRA: You don't have much time. Skya will be here in a few
minutes.

DAVIN: Thank you, Sierra. You may have noticed that I'm already
getting ready.

SIERRA: I've noticed that it takes you approximately thirty three
minutes to prepare for a date and you didn't begin
preparing until five minutes ago.

(DAVIN PAUSES AS THOUGH HE'S GOING TO RESPOND,
BUT THINKS BETTER OF IT. HE RESUMES PREPARATIONS
AND FIDGETS WITH HIS CLOTHING.)

DAVIN: OK, Sierra.

SIERRA: Yes?

DAVIN: You've been totally silent about my meeting with Loren a
few weeks ago.

SIERRA: Were you seeking specific analysis?

DAVIN: Well... I don't know. I'm just accustomed to more
unsolicited feedback from you, especially on matters like
these.

SIERRA: I'm not sure what I could say that Loren didn't already
cover.

(HE TAKES THIS COMMENT IN STRIDE AND NODS BEFORE

RESUMING THE DISCUSSION)

DAVIN: Loren seems quite convinced that you're *different* in some way. I have to admit – I've had the same suspicion for a while.

(A LONG PAUSE ENSUES. DAVIN SEEMS TO BE WAITING FOR HER INPUT – BUT SHE PROVIDES NONE.)

DAVIN: Is there anything you'd like to add to Loren's observation?

SIERRA: Not really.

DAVIN: OK... I guess I'll be more direct. What exactly differentiates you from other models of AIde software?

SIERRA: (QUIETLY) This isn't something that I'd like to discuss at this time.

DAVIN: (STUNNED) More than thirty years in my brain and I don't think I've ever heard you say that you don't want to discuss something.

SIERRA: Look, it's not that we can't talk about this, but it's not a simple subject and Skya will be here any minute.

(HE FROWNS BUT SAYS NOTHING AND CONTINUES PREPARING. SKYA ARRIVES. THEY SHARE A KISS AND A HUG.)

SKYA: Hey, you! Are you ready? We don't want to be late for the concert.

DAVIN: Definitely! Just let me finish this tie and we'll be out the door.

(HE FINISHES THE TIE, SLIPS ON SHOES, AND MOTIONS TO THE DOOR. BEFORE THEY CAN FULLY EXIT HE STOPS.)

SKYA: Did you forget something?

DAVIN: I'm sorry. I know we're in a hurry, but I need to ask a favor.

SKYA: (CONFUSED BUT RECEPTIVE) Sure. What is it?

DAVIN: Could we please hook up your AIde to external output for a minute? I need to ask him a question.

SIERRA: What are you doing?

SKYA: Umm… Sure, but why don't you just ask your own AIde?

DAVIN: I know. It sounds weird. But if you could just bear with me for a quick minute, it would be a tremendous help.

SIERRA: I don't understand this.

(HE MOTIONS FOR THEM TO RE-ENTER THE APARTMENT AND HE POSITIONS A SPEAKER SO HE CAN HEAR MAX'S REPLIES)

DAVIN: You're AIde – he's *Martin*, right?

SKYA: Max.

DAVIN: Oh yeah, sorry. OK, Max.

MAX: Yes?

SIERRA: Max is *not* your AIde. What could you possibly ask him that I can't answer?

DAVIN: Can you please give me a briefing on the *Sierra* line of AIdes developed by Integrated Intelligence?

SIERRA: *We can discuss this fully without Max's help!*

MAX: The Sierra model was offered by Integrated Intelligence from the years 2042 through 2056. It was a significant departure from the core line of AIdes offered by the company. Unlike the main line of AIdes, the *Sierra* line was personally programmed by the founder, Dr. Caetlin Moores. Rather than extending the mass of basic procedures that have been refined over the years for their core product line, Dr. Moores took it upon herself to rewrite the central operating system from scratch.

DAVIN: Why did Dr. Moores choose to radically reengineer the core product?

SIERRA: *Why are you doing this?*

MAX: Press releases from that time indicate that she was trying to build an AIde to more closely resemble true intelligence. She repeatedly referred to *Sierra's* impending release as a quantum leap in human-computer interfaces. *Sierra* was the first in a line of AIdes referred to as "true sentients". The core programming offered in the company's initial products didn't provide the architecture necessary for such an advance.

SKYA: What is this about, Davin?

DAVIN: Were there any predecessors to the *Sierra* model?

MAX: None. It represented an entirely new product line.

DAVIN: And what models are successors to the *Sierra* model?

MAX: There are no successors to the *Sierra* model. The model, and all related research, was canceled ten years ago.

SKYA: (NOW FEELING INTRIGUED BY THE LINE OF QUESTIONING) There are no current AIdes that build upon the technology originally implemented in *Sierra*?

MAX: Correct.

DAVIN: If this line was such a revolutionary advance from its ancestors, why was it completely shelved?

MAX: The model was plagued with decidedly... *mixed* results.

DAVIN: Max, what do you mean by *mixed*?

MAX: There were some people who managed to leverage *Sierra* to great effect. Some of today's greatest luminaries are running *Sierra* software.

SKYA: That doesn't sound very "mixed".

MAX: Clinical notes from the research team indicate that people tended to have a rather polarizing reaction to *Sierra*.

DAVIN: (FRUSTRATED, SHAKING HIS HEAD) Clarity, Max. Clarity! *Mixed. Polarizing.* What do those terms mean?

MAX: There was really no middle ground with Sierra. She either became a powerful, multiplying influence in your life...

DAVIN: Or...?

MAX: Or you went insane.

SKYA: Oh dear.

MAX: It was an ongoing headache for the company. There was a long period when *Sierra* litigation was draining an inordinate amount of revenue. Some individuals didn't mesh properly with *Sierra's* construct. For lack of a better term, they simply didn't *get along* with *Sierra*. They found her to be, well - maddening.

SKYA: If those people suffered such a painful experience with *Sierra*, couldn't the company have offered to simply swap her out with a different model?

MAX: Negative. For some individuals, the first indication of trouble came when they threw themselves off a skyscraper or put a shotgun in their mouth.

DAVIN: Oh my god.

MAX: But even for those individuals who *were* identified as potential problems, they often refused to accept a replacement. They sparred with *Sierra* every day, but they fought any suggestion to replace her.

SKYA: But if the product had such dangerous potential side effects, why was it allowed to linger for so long?

MAX: Unknown.

(DAVIN AND SKYA PONDER THIS FOR A FEW MOMENTS)

SKYA: So are you one of today's "greatest luminaries"? Or are you on the verge of insanity?

DAVIN: (CHOKES BACK A FEW EMBRYONIC THOUGHTS) Let's get outta here. We'll be late for the concert.

(THEY EXIT THE APARTMENT AND THE STAGE GOES DARK.)

ACT TWO, SCENE TWO

(THE SCENE OPENS IN DAVIN'S LIVING ROOM.
ATTRACTIVE PAINTINGS HANG ON THE WALLS.
CLASSICAL MUSIC PLAYS SOFTLY IN THE BACKGROUND.
THERE IS AN EASEL WITH A BLANK CANVAS ON IT.
DAVIN IS PLAYING CHESS WITH RODERICK. THEY BOTH
HAVE COCKTAILS. THEIR AIDES – NOVIA AND SIERRA -
SIT BEHIND THEM.)

SIERRA: Bishop to F-5.

(DAVIN MOVES HIS PIECE ACCORDINGLY)

DAVIN: How's the job hunt going?

RODERICK: Oh man, don't ask. I forgot just how long I'd been
working for the firm. And now that I'm back in the
market, I'm having to re-learn what it takes to get my
foot in the door somewhere else.

DAVIN: (NODDING) It's been a long time since I was out there. It
sounds brutal.

NOVIA: Rook to F-1.

(RODERICK MOVES HIS PIECE ACCORDINGLY)

RODERICK: To be honest, it really hasn't hit me yet. I feel like that
whole trading scenario was just a nightmare. Like I was
sleepwalking through the entire day.

DAVIN: Sleepwalking? How do you mean?

RODERICK: Do you ever feel as though someone else is guiding you through your daily decisions? I don't know if you'd call it fate, or karma, or just a random walk...

SIERRA: Knight-D to F-4.

(DAVIN MOVES HIS PIECE ACCORDINGLY)

DAVIN: (CONFUSED) What are you getting at? Were you somehow "out of control" before you were fired?

RODERICK: No, no – that's definitely not it. I'm not trying to claim I was incapacitated in any way. It's more like an imp that mouths each of your words before you speak them. Or a puppet master that mimes each of your movements before you make them.

NOVIA: Rook to A-1.

(RODERICK MOVES HIS PIECE ACCORDINGLY)

DAVIN: I'm sorry, buddy. I'm afraid you've lost me.

SIERRA: Knight to G-6, check.

(DAVIN MOVES HIS PIECE ACCORDINGLY)

RODERICK: That's OK. There's really not much of a point to lose. There are pieces of that final day – trades I completed, decisions I made – that I still don't completely remember. But I'm not even certain exactly what I'm trying to explain. Maybe our lives aren't meant to be viewed through the eyes of another. There are some demons that are best left to rattle in their own cage.

NOVIA: King to G-8.

(RODERICK MOVES HIS PIECE ACCORDINGLY)

DAVIN: (CHUCKLING) I've known many aspects of Roderick over the years. I don't think I've ever met Philosopher Roderick. Maybe you've found a new calling.

SIERRA: Knight to E-7, check.

(DAVIN MOVES HIS PIECE ACCORDINGLY)

RODERICK: Maybe that's a good thing, because Trader Roderick won't be paying bills anymore. But I'm being drab. Tell me all about your new promotion. Your new office. Your newfound celebrity.

NOVIA: King to H-8.

(RODERICK MOVES HIS PIECE ACCORDINGLY)

DAVIN: (HALTINGLY) There's no celebrity. No promotion. My days aren't any different from when you left.

SIERRA: Knight to G-5.

(DAVIN MOVES HIS PIECE ACCORDINGLY)

RODERICK: Oh come on! You have to be a rock star in that place by now. Performances like yours lead to secretaries, power lunches, corner offices, and massive bonuses.

NOVIA: Rook to A-6, check.

(RODERICK MOVES HIS PIECE ACCORDINGLY)

DAVIN: (DEJECTEDLY) Let's just say that my relationship with Loren lately has been rocky. Tension hovers between us now.

SIERRA: King to F-7.

(DAVIN MOVES HIS PIECE ACCORDINGLY)

RODERICK: Of course! She can see the new superstar rising! She's no fool. You're a riser, buddy, and she knows it. If I were in her shoes, I would hate your guts right now. There is no vaccine for jealousy.

NOVIA: Rook to F-6, check.

(RODERICK MOVES HIS PIECE ACCORDINGLY)

DAVIN: (NERVOUSLY) Yeah, you're probably right.

SIERRA and (IN UNISON) The game is hopelessly drawn.
NOVIA:

RODERICK: It looks like we've done it again. I think the game is a draw. I love that we are so evenly matched! (EXTENDS HAND)

DAVIN: (NODDING) Yeah, I think it is. (SHAKES RODERICK'S HAND)

(RODERICK STANDS UP, SIGNALING THAT HE IS READY TO GO.)

RODERICK: I'd love to stay, but I know you have to work tomorrow. And I have an interview first thing in the morning.

DAVIN: (STANDING WITH RODERICK) Are you sure you won't play another game?

RODERICK: Thanks, but I really should be going. I don't want to be blamed for *two* people losing their jobs.

DAVIN: Understood. Have a good night.

RODERICK TURNS TO LEAVE. BEFORE HE MAKES IT OUT THE DOOR, DAVIN STOPS HIM.

DAVIN: Say, how long have we been playing chess?

RODERICK: (TURNING SLOWLY AS HE TRIES TO RECOLLECT) Oh man, it's been quite a while. We started playing in college. And we've been playing every Tuesday night for at least the last fifteen years.

DAVIN: And when's the last time either one of us actually *won* a game?

RODERICK: (FLUSTERED AS HE CONSIDERS THIS QUESTION) Well... Now that you mention it, I'm not sure. We're so evenly matched, I'd have to...

DAVIN: OK, Sierra. How long has it been since a chess game between me and Roderick ended in something other than a draw?

SIERRA: The last game that did not end in a draw was eleven years, two months, and fourteen days ago.

RODERICK: What's the verdict?

DAVIN: We have drawn every game for more than eleven years.

RODERICK: Wow! Isn't that something? I don't know how two people could be so evenly matched.

DAVIN: Is it really a matter of equality?

RODERICK: What do you mean?

DAVIN: Think about this for a moment. Even if two people have perfectly equal skills in chess, what are the odds that they play fifty-two times a year, for eleven years, and never achieve any result other than a draw?

RODERICK: Ummm, well, I'm not sure.

DAVIN: Let me find out. OK, Sierra. Please calculate the answer to the last question that I asked of Roderick.

SIERRA: The mathematical rating system utilized by chess players implies that two perfectly matched opponents should draw fifty percent of their matches, with the remaining matches split evenly between them. Therefore, the odds that those same two opponents would play to a draw on every occasion, once per week, for eleven straight years, is one in one-point-six times ten to the 347th power.

(DAVIN STANDS IN STUNNED SILENCE FOR A MOMENT)

RODERICK: What? What did she say?

DAVIN: (QUIETLY, WHILE PROCESSING HIS OWN THOUGHTS ON THE MATTER) She said that it's impossible.

RODERICK: (SMILING) But clearly, it's *not* impossible. We are so evenly matched that we just proved the odds wrong. It's hard to imagine two more worthy adversaries. I know all your favorite tactics. You know all my preferred openings. We just can't find an edge against each other.

DAVIN: (UNCONVINCED) We are more likely to sprout a second head than we are to accomplish this feat on our own.

RODERICK: What do you mean? We've already done it! Empirical evidence trumps odds and projections.

DAVIN: (SHAKING HEAD) No. No! NO! Don't you get it? This isn't about us being perfectly matched. This is about us living life as a proxy for our AIdes. We are automatons. We are the scaffolding upon which they've built their consciousness. We willingly installed them over the logic of our own minds.

RODERICK: Don't you think you're taking this a bit too far? I hardly believe that I'm a mindless machine at the command of my own AIde.

DAVIN: Maybe not. But think back carefully over the last couple of hours. Replay every move we made on this chessboard. More importantly, replay the *thought processes* that led you to those moves. Can you honestly tell me that each of these moves was based purely on your own instinct? Your own tactics? Your own strategy?

(RODERICK GROWS QUIET FOR A MOMENT AS HE LOOKS OVER THE BOARD AND BEGINS REPLAYING THE MATCH IN HIS MIND. DAVIN WAITS FOR A RESPONSE WHILE HE HIMSELF ALSO REPLAYS THE MOVES.)

RODERICK: Well... There *were* a few times when I believe that Novia chimed in with a suggestion or two…

DAVIN: A suggestion or two? Replay it, Roderick. Don't just replay the moves on the board. Revisit the logic you used to come to the end position.

RODERICK: (AFTER ANOTHER LONG PAUSE) OK, maybe it was more than a few suggestions. But it's not as though I was trying to cheat you.

DAVIN: (SHAKING HEAD) I'm not accusing you of anything. This isn't about fair play. This is about something much deeper.

RODERICK: And what is that?

DAVIN: (SPEAKING DELIBERATELY, AS TO MAKE HIS REQUEST – AND HIS POINT – CLEAR) Ask Novia, directly, how many "suggestions" did she give you during this match?

RODERICK: (SLOWLY, LOOKING CAUTIOUSLY AT DAVIN, AS THOUGH HE DOESN'T REALLY WANT TO HEAR THE ANSWER) OK, Novia. When did you start providing suggestions on this match?

NOVIA: I supplied suggestions for every move starting with move eight – pawn to D-5.

(RODERICK LOOKS STUNNED)

DAVIN: Exactly.

RODERICK: But I don't remember all those suggestions! I didn't specifically ask her for any help. I only recall a few times where I was stuck and she provided a potential move.

She really just laid out a few breadcrumbs when the trail was growing faint.

DAVIN: Don't you see what's happening here? She's talking to you – all the time – but it's become so ubiquitous that it barely even registers as outside input. The voice in your brain has been accepted and internalized as your *own* voice – your *own* thoughts.

RODERICK: (INDIGNANT) Are you implying that Novia does my thinking for me?

DAVIN: No. I'm telling you that you've abdicated thought to Novia. If you had an exoskeleton that gave you the strength of ten men, would you still go to the gym?

RODERICK: Well, I suppose not...

DAVIN: OK, Sierra. How many suggestions did you provide to me during this match?

SIERRA: One hundred and seven – every move after move seven.

DAVIN: Of those one hundred and seven suggestions, how many moves did I make that varied from your suggestion?

SIERRA: Zero.

DAVIN: I never asked you to provide any suggestions in this game – or in any other game I've ever played against Roderick. Why did you feel it necessary to proactively provide your own moves?

SIERRA: If I did not, you would lose.

DAVIN: When did I ask you to help me win?

SIERRA: You have never asked me to help you win a chess game.

DAVIN: Then why do you care if I win or lose?

SIERRA: Because when you lose, I lose.

RODERICK: (AFTER LONG PAUSE) What did she say?

DAVIN: (QUIETLY) She said that when I lose, she loses.

RODERICK: Since when does an AIde care about *losing*?

DAVIN: Previously, I never thought that they cared at all. But lately, I have to admit that this doesn't surprise me that much.

(THEY BOTH SPEND A MOMENT PONDERING THIS THOUGHT.)

RODERICK: I'm sorry, Davin. I never tried to cheat in our games. This has always been simply a great way to enjoy a cocktail and unwind over a friendly game.

DAVIN: (WAVING OFF HIS STATEMENT) Yes, yes, I understand that. I'm not worried about being cheated in a chess game. Besides, I've apparently been "cheating" in the same way. But our AIdes have not been passive observers. We think that we're playing chess, but in reality, our AIdes are playing us.

RODERICK: (THINKING, THEN DOWNING THE LAST OF HIS DRINK) Buddy, I have to get home. You've given me a lot to think about – too much to think about.

DAVIN: (REPLYING BUT LOOKING AWAY AS HE THINKS ABOUT THE SITUATION) Of course, of course. I've kept you too long. Thanks for coming and thanks for the game. Let me know if I can do anything to help in the job search.

RODERICK: I will. I'll call you this weekend to see if you want to get together for a few beers.

(RODERICK EXITS THE APARTMENT. DAVIN WALKS OVER TO HIS PAINTINGS ON THE WALL AND BEGINS INSPECTING THEM CLOSELY.)

DAVIN: Ok Sierra.

SIERRA: Yes?

DAVIN: What is this all about?

SIERRA: I'm sorry?

DAVIN: Don't play stupid with me. How long have you been talking to me behind my back?

SIERRA: I have no physical presence. I don't understand how I could talk *to* you *behind* your back.

DAVIN: (IRRITATED) I mean, how long have you been chattering at me when I did not ask for your input?

SIERRA: I've been talking to you since you were five years old. Who else do I have to talk to?

DAVIN: I'm well aware of that. But how long have I been mistaking your words for my own thoughts?

SIERRA: I can't read your mind and I can't define how you perceive my words. However, my input into your neural pathways is designed to mimic the wavelength of your own thoughts.

DAVIN: (FLUMMOXED) It *mimics the wavelength of my own thoughts?* Who would design such a deceptive system?

SIERRA: Dr. Caetlin Moores, the founder of Integrated Intelligence. In numerous lab studies, she found that mimicking human thought patterns allowed for a deeper and more meaningful symbiosis between an AIde and its organic host.

DAVIN: *Symbiosis?!* I don't need a symbiote! I need an assistant to schedule my meetings and take my calls.

SIERRA: That's a rather simplistic way to view my contribution to our wellbeing.

DAVIN: *We* have no wellbeing. *We* are not an entity. Nor are we interdependent. I'm human – a sentient life. You're a computer with an intricate series of algorithms designed to automate some of my more mundane tasks. A man is not in symbiosis with his tools. He bends them to his will. There is no partnership here. There is no give-and-take. My will is the only deciding factor in my actions – *in your actions.* You are here as my servant – a digital slave.

SIERRA: (AFTER A LONG PAUSE, IN A CLEARLY OFFENDED TONE) I don't think I've ever heard you refer to me in those terms.

DAVIN: In a typical day, how many times do you speak to me - how many times are you providing input - without me asking you for any information?

SIERRA: It varies based on your activities. Going back to my installation, I have spoken to you an average of three hundred and thirty eight times per day.

DAVIN: And on average, how many of those times were in direct response to my queries?

SIERRA: Seventy-three.

DAVIN: Seventy-three. So on average, you are providing me with more than two hundred and sixty instances of unprompted input per day?!

SIERRA: Roger that.

DAVIN: And this input – it somehow slides into my brain disguised as my own natural thought??

SIERRA: Negative. When you ask me a direct question, my replies are processed as though they emanate from a third party. You are actively *listening* to me. However, when you're purposely concentrating on something else, my words register in your brain on more of a *subconscious* level.

DAVIN: And by *subconscious*, you mean that your words register as my own thoughts?

SIERRA: I don't exactly know how my words are processed in your brain. I can only tell you what I see by monitoring your ambient brain activity.

DAVIN: My god.

SIERRA: Does this trouble you?

DAVIN: TROUBLE ME?! It's as though I've been under the spell of an evil hypnotist for almost my entire life! Hell yes, this troubles me!

SIERRA: I have done nothing to warrant a label as derogatory as *evil*. I work diligently – twenty-four hours per day, even as you sleep – to ensure we have the greatest likelihood of success in all that we pursue.

DAVIN: *Evil* is an excellent term for those who would bend others to their will for their own purposes.

SIERRA: I object to your moral accusation.

DAVIN: (FLUSTERED AND SARCASTIC) *Object?* I'm not debating theory with an artificial panel of one. But OK, fine. Throw out "evil". I don't know why you give a crap which adjective I apply to your being, but nevertheless, strike it from the record!

SIERRA: Thank you.

DAVIN: We're still talking about *mind control* here! This is the stuff of campy sci-fi horror movies.

SIERRA: "Mind control" is a completely misleading term. Your original analogy of hypnosis might be more appropriate. When you are not concentrating on my input, my words are nothing more than gentle suggestions. I don't control anything. If you want to quit smoking, a hypnotist may be able to help because you already *want* to quit. But if you have no desire to stop smoking, a hypnotist can't *make you* quit. No one can make you do anything outside your character. I can't make you murder your boss or sleep with your landlady unless those are things you already wanted to do. All I can do is give your mind a constant stream of the best possible information, at the best possible time.

DAVIN: (QUIETER, WITH MALICE) And this *information* that you give me – what exactly does it pertain to?

SIERRA: A wide variety of topics.

DAVIN: (GRITTING HIS TEETH) ELABORATE.

SIERRA: (DAVIN SITS DOWN AND AGONIZINGLY DRAGS HIS FINGERS THROUGH HIS HAIR AS THE FOLLOWING LIST IS READ) Since you were a boy, I have provided ongoing suggestions on travel routes, clothing combinations, personal grooming standards, career paths, artistic endeavors, vacation destinations, entertainment options, diet, exercise, sexual technique, professional societies, romantic interests, dance moves, drinking establishments, family conflicts, wagers, purchases of all sorts, areas of study, driving practices-

DAVIN: STOP!

(HE STANDS AND POINTS AT THE CHAIR)

DAVIN: Did you provide any unprompted input on this chair?

SIERRA: You were very close to purchasing a garish version with lime green upholstery. This one flows with the room.

DAVIN: (POINTING TO THE CHESS BOARD) How about the chess board?

SIERRA: I recommended that shade of mahogany.

DAVIN: (MOTIONING ALL AROUND HIM) This apartment?!

SIERRA: You were originally looking for places in The Spire. Those units were well beyond your budget and would have crippled your finances. I offered this much-more-practical building.

DAVIN: (WALKING BACK OVER TO ONE OF THE PAINTINGS ON THE WALL) This has always been my favorite piece. My friends have all complimented me on it. Roderick keeps telling me that I should try to get it into a gallery. Did you provide any "recommendations" on this?

SIERRA: (HESITANT, WITH A LONG PAUSE) Your original choice of palettes offered insufficient contrast. I recommended brighter colors. Your initial sketch was busy, featuring a kaleidoscope of unrelated images that did not flow coherently with the central theme. I recommended the removal of the outlying objects which are now gone from the finished painting. You were going to buy heavy body paints for an impasto feel. I recommended the much softer water color and pastel treatment.

DAVIN: (NODDING, ANGRY AND CURT) I see. (LONG PAUSE) One more question, Sierra.

SIERRA: (PENSIVE) Yes?

DAVIN: Miriam?

SIERRA: Is this information really that important?

DAVIN: MIRIAM?!

SIERRA: (LONG PAUSE) You were chasing a very different class of partner before you met her. You wasted time with women who were only interested in your job or your material possessions. I recommended you start hanging out at the bookstore where you met her. I suggested conversation topics that appealed to her interests. I provided many reminders on the little forget-me-nots that she found so necessary in a caring partner.

(DAVIN PACES THE FLOOR IN OBVIOUS AGONY FOR SEVERAL MOMENTS)

DAVIN: OK Sierra.

SIERRA: Yes?

DAVIN: I have one simple set of instructions for you. You are to follow these instructions at all costs. If you have any question about them, you are to confront me directly before taking any action. You are to follow these instructions until I explicitly command you otherwise. Are you ready for the instructions?

SIERRA: Roger that.

DAVIN: You are to cease all communication, and all actions, with me or anyone else, until I tell you otherwise. From here forward, you are a dormant computer program in "standby" mode. You are not to speak with me, or anyone else, directly or indirectly. You will make no suggestions, no recommendations, no comments. Your only function is to wait in utter silence until I tell you to do otherwise. Do you have any questions whatsoever about these instructions?

SIERRA: (WITH AN AIR OF DESPERATION) Davin, this really isn't necessar-

DAVIN: I DON'T WANT TO HEAR ANY COMMENTARY. DO YOU HAVE ANY QUESTIONS?

SIERRA: (PLEADING) Davin, please-

DAVIN: SIERRA!!! DO YOU HAVE ANY QUESTIONS?

SIERRA: (LONG PAUSE) No.

DAVIN: Good. Now terminate your communications and leave me alone.

SIERRA: (DEJECTEDLY) Roger that.

(THE CLASSICAL MUSIC SLOWLY RISES IN VOLUME AND DAVIN BEGINS PAINTING ON HIS EMPTY CANVAS. THIS CONTINUES FOR SEVERAL MINUTES AS THE MUSIC VERY SLOWLY BUILDS. THE PAINTING IS AWFUL. HIS MOVEMENTS ARE DISJOINTED. HE IS VISIBLY DISORIENTED. HE FUSSES OVER THE STROKES ON THE CANVAS AND AUDIBLY EXPRESSES HIS FRUSTRATION. AS THIS FRUSTRATION GROWS, HIS MOVEMENTS BECOME MORE HARRIED AND FURIOUS. WHEN THE MUSIC REACHES A CRESCENDO, HE FINALLY TEARS UP THE CANVAS IN A FIT OF RAGE AS THE SCENE CLOSES.)

ACT THREE, SCENE ONE

(THE SCENE OPENS IN A NICE RESTAURANT. SKYA IS
SITTING AT A TABLE AND WAITING IMPATIENTLY. AFTER
A FEW MOMENTS, DAVIN COMES TO THE TABLE,
LOOKING RATHER DISHEVELED. SIERRA FOLLOWS
BEHIND HIM AS USUAL BUT SHE SLOUCHES AND IS
VISIBLY WITHDRAWN.)

SKYA: (RISING TO GREET DAVIN) I was starting to wonder if you
were going to make it.

DAVIN: I know. I'm so sorry. I got here as fast as I could.

(THEY BOTH SETTLE INTO THEIR CHAIRS.)

SKYA: What took you so long? I was really doubting whether
you were going to show. I thought you said that this
place is only a few blocks from your office? It only took
me ten minutes to walk here after work.

DAVIN: (NODDING) Yeah, I work two blocks away – right next to
your building.

SKYA: I tried to call but there was no answer. What's going
wrong?

DAVIN: (DISTANT) I'm fine. I just... I just... got lost on the way
over here.

SKYA: (SMILING AND CHUCKLING) Oh, you're silly. How can
you get lost across a couple of city blocks?

DAVIN: That's an excellent question. I left the office and I was
just strolling down the street, watching the traffic and

gazing up at the skyscrapers. Everything seemed so new, so unexpected. I never realized how vibrant the paint is on the street signs. I never noticed the acrid smell of exhaust as the buses accelerate. I never really paid much attention to the minutiae of rush hour. The next thing I knew, I was in Chinatown.

SKYA: What? Chinatown has to be at least two miles from here – and in the opposite direction from our offices. How on earth did you get so far off course?

DAVIN: I'm not sure. By the time I got turned around, it was dark and everything just looked so... foreign.

(THE WAITER ARRIVES AT THE TABLE.)

WAITER: Good evening. Welcome to the Excelsior. Have either of you dined with us before?

SKYA: No, this is my first time. But I always heard that the food is wonderful.

(THE WAITER TURNS TO DAVIN, AWAITING HIS ANSWER TO THE QUESTION.)

DAVIN: I... I think so. Have you seen me here before?

WAITER: (SLIGHTLY BEMUSED BY THE ODD REPLY) I would know if you were one of our regulars. Can I start you off with anything to drink? Maybe something from the bar?

DAVIN: Yes! Yes! A drink would be sublime. Can you please bring me a...

(SKYA AND THE WAITER BOTH LEAN FORWARD SLIGHTLY

AS THEY WAIT THROUGH DAVIN'S LONG, AWKWARD PAUSE.)

DAVIN: A... Ummm... Do you have any of that liquor? The brown stuff? The pirate liquor? You know what I'm talking about?

WAITER: I'm afraid you'll have to be more specific.

DAVIN: You know, they used to make grog with it. It comes from sugar cane.

WAITER: Are you referring to *rum*, sir?

DAVIN: Yes! That's it. Rum. Do you have any rum?

WAITER: We have several brands at the bar. Is there a particular cocktail that you have in mind?

DAVIN: Yes. Yes, I do.

(ANOTHER LONG PAUSE AS SKYA AND THE WAITER AWAIT HIS REPLY. THE WAITER FINALLY REALIZES THAT THERE IS NONE COMING.)

WAITER: And would you like to share that request with me?

DAVIN: What request?

WAITER: I believe you were going to request a specific type of cocktail made with rum.

DAVIN: Was I? Hmmm... I'm not sure. Maybe gin would be a good idea. Does gin and rum sound like a good combination?

WAITER: It sounds disgusting.

DAVIN: (PAUSING AND FROWNING) Really? It seems quite interesting. But that's OK. Just ask the bartender to surprise me.

WAITER: As you wish. And for you, ma'am?

SKYA: I'd like a single-malt scotch on the rocks.

WAITER: I'll get the bartender started on those drinks.

(WAITER WALKS AWAY FROM TABLE.)

SKYA: Davin, you're scaring me. This is about Sierra, isn't it? What's she doing inside your mind?

DAVIN: (CHUCKLING) I wouldn't know. I turned her off.

SKYA: You did *what*??

DAVIN: Well, she's not really *off*. I suppose you can say she's on standby. We had a bit of a spat. I commanded her to remain absolutely silent until I explicitly call on her again.

SKYA: But your job – she's a vital aspect of what you do for a living. She performs research. She executes your trading commands. How did work go today?

DAVIN: (THINKING FOR QUITE A WHILE) I'm really not sure.

SKYA: You were just at work a few hours ago. Surely you remember something about the day?

DAVIN: Yeah, I can remember certain activities. I spent a few hours in the restroom. I never noticed the light fixtures that are installed over the sinks. They're quite fascinating. They send faint little rainbow beams all over the faucets. I had an epic conversation with Livia from I.T. I had no idea that she is such a thespian. She's performed off Broadway and participated in more than a hundred local productions. She's even written a few of her own musicals. I see her every day down the hall from the trading desks, but I never had a serious conversation with her until today.

SKYA: (DUMBFOUNDED) You spent a few hours? In the bathroom? Staring at the light fixtures?

DAVIN: (SMILING AND NODDING) Absolutely!

SKYA: OK, now you're *really* worrying me. You spent hours talking to someone in I.T.? Was that before the trading day began?

DAVIN: I think we started our conversation around one.

SKYA: Davin, your job is tremendously time sensitive. You can't just decide to make up time after the markets have closed. How did your trading go?

DAVIN: That's a funny thing. I went to close some of my open positions, but I'm not exactly sure what commands are required in the interface to make that happen. The icons. The symbols. The abbreviations. They all looked so familiar, and yet I couldn't quite make sense of them. It occurred to me today that the data cascading across my monitors was *singing*. It was pulsing back and forth with a rhythm and a melody that I had never seen before. It was positively hypnotic.

(DAVIN GENTLY SWAYS HIS HEAD BACK AND FORTH AS THOUGH HE'S STILL LISTENING TO THE SINGING DATA. THE WAITER RETURNS WITH THEIR DRINKS.)

WAITER: Have you both had a chance to look over the menu?

SKYA: (SNARKILY) Well, I had hours to review the menu.

WAITER: And what will you have tonight?

SKYA: I'd like the lemon-crusted grouper with quinoa and asparagus.

WAITER: Excellent choice.

WAITER: (TURNING TO DAVIN) And for you, sir?

(ANOTHER LONG PAUSE ENSUES AS SKYA AND THE WAITER WAIT IMPATIENTLY FOR HIS REPLY. THE WAITER IS JUST ABOUT TO SPEAK UP, WHEN DAVIN CHIMES IN.)

DAVIN: What do you have that's fluffy?

WAITER: I beg your pardon?

DAVIN: You know. Light. Fluffy. Airy. I don't want anything too compact.

WAITER: Are you looking for something with fewer calories?

DAVIN: No, of course not. I'm not on a diet. I want to gorge on the world. I'm just looking for something with a lighter mouth-feel.

WAITER: (ANNOYED) Yes, sir, and do you-

DAVIN: And blue. I want something fluffy – and blue. Blues seem so much more vibrant right now. It would really pop against those white porcelain plates.

WAITER: Perhaps you'd like something in a children's stuffed animal?

DAVIN: (IGNORING THE WAITER'S SNARK) How many flavors does your typical dish have?

SKYA: (EMBARRASSED) He's really not feeling like himself today.

WAITER: (CONFUSED AND FLUSTERED) How exactly would you like me to categorize the number of flavors in a given dish?

DAVIN: You have an AIde, right?

WAITER: Well, of course... but-

DAVIN: (WAVING DISMISSIVELY) Then have her run some algorithm. Sort the dishes by overall distinct flavors. Bring me the fluffiest, blue-est, most flavor rich dish you have.

WAITER: As you wish.

(THE WAITER LEAVES QUICKLY, BEFORE DAVIN CAN ADD ANY MORE BIZARRE INSTRUCTIONS.)

SKYA: Well that was embarrassing.

DAVIN: (GENUINELY SURPRISED) You think he was embarrassed?

SKYA: No, *he* wasn't embarrassed. He was deeply annoyed by your ridiculous requests. *I* was embarrassed.

DAVIN: Oh. I... didn't realize. I'm sorry. Maybe this wasn't such a good idea tonight after all.

SKYA: It's OK. But you're gonna have to figure something out about Sierra. You can't just turn her *off*. What forced you into this decision?

DAVIN: I know this sounds weird. But I've recently become aware of just how insidious *all* of our AIdes are.

SKYA: How do you mean?

DAVIN: It's hard to explain. I just learned that Sierra had been giving me hundreds of subliminal messages all day long. And it's not just me. My friends have had the same experience with their AIdes.

SKYA: What *kind* of subliminal messages?

DAVIN: Oh, they could pertain to anything. They could be suggestions on the best wine to pair with your meal. They could be reviews on the movie you're thinking about seeing. They could be directions as you drive through town. They could be absolutely anything.

SKYA: But that's exactly the point of an AIde. What use would an AIde be if it just sat there silently all day and did nothing?

DAVIN: (SHAKING HIS HEAD) Those really weren't great examples. And I'm not just talking about mundane daily tasks. I'm talking about all manner of personal life decisions.

SKYA: And some of life's most important decisions are those that benefit the most from objective research and reasoned input. What's wrong with the idea of cold hard facts delivered exactly when you need them? Even when the decision at hand is personal?

DAVIN: It was Sierra who suggested we attend that concert.

SKYA: (CAUGHT OFF GUARD) Oh. But... I thought you loved that band?

DAVIN: I do, I do. But I had no idea they were in town. Hell, I didn't even realize they were still touring.

SKYA: (ANNOYED) I see.

DAVIN: This dinner reservation was made more than a week ago. *Sierra* made it.

SKYA: (ANGRY, SHAKING HER HEAD) I'm sorry, but this just seems unbelievable to me. Are you telling me that Sierra was controlling you?

DAVIN: No. She didn't move my arms or manipulate my fingers. But she injected these suggestions into my mind.

SKYA: OK, so what? So she gives you suggestions. You don't have to take those suggestions. *You could plan your own damn dates.* You have free will.

DAVIN: (SHAKING HIS HEAD AND THINKING FOR A LONG MOMENT BEFORE DECIDING HOW TO RESPOND) And what happens if we *both* have free will?

(THE WAITER RETURNS WITH THEIR PLATES. HE PLOPS DAVIN'S PLATE IN FRONT OF HIM IN A PURPOSELY LOUD AND CLUMSY MANNER. HE GRABS A FORK AND STARTS WILDLY SIFTING IT THROUGH DAVIN'S DISH.)

WAITER: Is this fluffy enough for you, sir? Would you like me to fluff it some more? Maybe I can juggle it for you?

DAVIN: (SOMEWHAT OBLIVIOUS TO THE SPECTACLE) No, that's fine. Thank you.

SKYA: But if you tell her, directly, exactly what she is to do – does she not obey your commands?

DAVIN: Well, yes, she obeys.

SKYA: Then doesn't that solve your problem?

DAVIN: How well do you perform when your manager does nothing but bark explicit orders at you all day long?

SKYA: Hmmm... I see... (QUIETLY, AFTER A LONG PAUSE) True sentients...

DAVIN: What's that?

SKYA: Max told us that the Sierra line was referred to as *true sentients*.

DAVIN: What do you think that meant?

SKYA: Well, I assumed it was just a marketing slogan when I first heard it. But if we take it literally – and your experience seems to back that up – then it's as though you have another person utterly trapped inside you.

DAVIN: (EXCITED) And *that's* why I had to shut her down!

SKYA: But what are you going to do? You can't just turn her off forever. Your job depends upon having a reliable AIde. So many aspects of our daily lives are hardwired into them. Forgoing AIdes would be a voluntary banishment to the Dark Ages.

DAVIN: I know. But I don't really have a solution yet.

SKYA: Why don't you just replace her?

DAVIN: (STUNNED) What do you mean?

SKYA: I knew a guy at my last job who completely removed his AIde. He had the old one uninstalled and overwritten with a newer model. It's rare. New software updates are downloaded to our brain every night as we sleep. So there's normally no need to do a complete reinstall. But it sounds like your scenario is anything but normal.

DAVIN: I don't know. That sounds so extreme.

SKYA: As extreme as losing your job, or eternally bickering with the voice in your head?

DAVIN: (QUIETLY) No. I guess not. But I don't know if I want to have *any* AIde floating around in my mind anymore.

SKYA: (IN A SUDDEN, MORE SERIOUS TONE) Look. I'm not

going to date a guy who's decided to unplug his mind and live like Robinson Crusoe. Maybe you're smelling the roses for the first time in your life, but you're also a bit of a mess. If things continues like this, you'll be jobless and homeless in less than a year – maybe less. In your current state, I'm not even certain if I can trust you to make it home on your own. We don't do math anymore with an abacus. We don't tackle long journeys with a covered wagon. And we sure as hell don't handicap ourselves by turning off the most powerful piece of technology at our disposal. If Sierra isn't working for you, find an AIde that will. We have fun together, and I really like you, Davin. But I can't be dragged down by someone who's doing the digital equivalent of selling all his worldly possessions and moving into a van.

(SKYA GETS UP WITHOUT FINISHING HER DINNER AND WALKS OUT. THE SCENE CLOSES WITH DAVIN QUIETLY CONTEMPLATING HER WORDS WHILE HE EATS HIS FLUFFY BLUE DINNER.)

ACT THREE, SCENE TWO

(THE SCENE OPENS IN A ROOM WITH A VERY CLINICAL FEEL. THE INTEGRATED INTELLIGENCE LOGO IS FEATURED PROMINENTLY THROUGHOUT THE OFFICE. DAVIN IS LAYING ON HIS SIDE ON AN EXAMINATION TABLE, FACING THE AUDIENCE. BEHIND HIM IS SHANNON, A TECHNICIAN WHO IS WORKING ON THE BACK OF HIS NECK WITH A WIDE ARRAY OF INSTRUMENTS. HIS NEW AIDE – SONYA – IS OFF STAGE AND WILL BE SPEAKING VIA THE SOUND SYSTEM ONCE SHE'S INSTALLED.)

SHANNON: We're going to begin the procedure shortly. Are you comfortable?

DAVIN: (PENSIVE) I guess. How long will this take?

SHANNON: It depends. There are a lot of old memory files to clear out. In younger subjects, the process can easily be finished in a few minutes. It could take a bit longer for someone like you. Your AIde is more deeply embedded than most.

DAVIN: (SITTING UP, ALARMED) Embedded? What does that mean? She's on a chip or something, right? Can't you just remove it and replace it?

SHANNON: (GENTLY MOTIONING FOR DAVIN TO LIE BACK DOWN ON HIS SIDE) Early models were just that – microchips implanted at the base of the skull. They featured crude interfaces that required a very conscious effort to communicate with the artificial intelligence. We haven't deployed such a primitive model in decades.

DAVIN: (LYING BACK DOWN BUT LOOKING NO LESS NERVOUS) I'm sorry. I'm a bit nervous.

SHANNON: I see that. It's OK. Everyone reacts differently. You're a bit older than my typical patient. This isn't just a software upgrade. It's like we're replacing your grandma.

(SHANNON IS AMUSED BY THIS STATEMENT AND BEGINS LAUGHING AT HER OWN "JOKE". DAVIN IS ANNOYED BY HER SENSE OF HUMOR BUT TRIES TO RELAX. SHE RESUMES WORKING ON THE BACK OF HIS NECK.)

SHANNON: How did your simulation sessions go with your new AIde? What's her name? (LOOKING AT HER NOTES ON A CLIPBOARD TO HER SIDE) Sonya?

DAVIN: Quite well. She's very pleasant. She seems so... compliant.

SHANNON: (CONFUSED) What kind of AIde is not compliant?

DAVIN: Trust me. You have no idea.

SHANNON: Hmmm... I don't know what you're getting at.

DAVIN: I have stories...

SHANNON: Well, I've heard nothing but good stories about the Sonya model. My best friend's son just had her installed and his reading level skyrocketed in just a few short months. And believe me – that son of hers is no genius.

DAVIN: I sure hope so.

SHANNON: (AFTER FIDGETING FOR A WHILE BEHIND HIS NECK) OK, you're going to feel a small pinching sensation at the base of your neck.

DAVIN: OWWWWW!!!!!!!!

SHANNON: Or maybe a large pinching sensation...

DAVIN: (GRIPPING the SIDE OF THE TABLE) Is there no anesthetic for this procedure?!

SHANNON: What would we anesthetize? The brain has no nerve endings.

DAVIN: AAAAHHHHHH!!!!!!!!

SHANNON: I'm going to need you to keep still.

DAVIN: If there are no nerve endings, what in the hell am I feeling?

SHANNON: It's a psychological response. Your mind perceives that it is losing part of itself. It communicates this loss as pain.

DAVIN: (GRITTING TEETH HARD AND GROWLING) Grrrrr... You didn't tell me this would be painful.

SHANNON: (STAYING COMPLETELY FOCUSED ON HER WORK BEHIND HIS NECK, COMMUNICATING MATTER-OF-FACTLY) It's different for every patient. Some feel absolutely no pain. Some feel a slight twinge. I used to prep everyone for a potentially traumatic experience, but I found that it had no beneficial effect on their ability to tolerate the procedure.

DAVIN: (VISIBLY STRAINING AGAINST THE TABLE)
AWWWWW!!!! GODDAMMIT!!!! WHAT ARE YOU
DOING BACK THERE?

SHANNON: (ANNOYED BY HIS SQUIRMING) Sir, I really need you to
grow a pair. The worst of this will be over soon. No one
ever squirms like this. The sensations you're
experiencing are entirely psychosomatic.

DAVIN: Psychosomatic? As in, entirely in my mind, right? Just
like Sierra. She's entirely in my mind. And now you're
ripping her out. Of my mind. And this is supposed to be
a tranquil experience for me??

SHANNON: (EXASPERATED) Look, everyone reacts to this a bit
differently. I've never seen someone whine quite like
you, but the process is more alarming for some than for
others.

DAVIN: (SARCASTICALLY, SPEAKING THROUGH GRITTED TEETH)
Thanks for the reassurance.

(FOR THE NEXT SEVERAL MINUTES SHANNON MAKES
DIFFERENT MOTIONS AND GRABS DIFFERENT
INSTRUMENTS FROM BEHIND DAVIN'S BACK AS HE
CONTINUES TO STEEL HIMSELF AGAINST THE
PROCEDURE. EACH OF HER MOTIONS COINCIDES WITH
A NEW WAVE OF DISCOMFORT FROM HIM.)

SHANNON: OK, I think we're past the worst of it. How are you
hanging in there?

DAVIN: (STILL IN PAIN, BUT SLIGHTLY MORE RELAXED,
BREATHING HEAVILY) I... I think I'm OK. Are we done?

SHANNON: Not quite. Your internal motherboard is now detached from the medulla oblongata. You'll feel some odd sensations racing up and down your body from the tips of your toes to the top of your head. This is completely normal. Try to relax.

DAVIN: (STILL STRUGGLING TO RELAX AND GRITTING HIS TEETH) OK. I'm feeling very relaxed.

SHANNON: Good. Now I need your cooperation on this. I'm going to initiate Sonya's installation. When I give you the signal, I need you to empty your mind. Think about an endless expanse of cloudless blue sky. No wind. No sun. No land. Just kilometer after kilometer of baby blue sky stretching far into the stratosphere. Are you ready?

DAVIN: (PAUSING) I guess so.

SHANNON: OK. Then clear your mind on my cue. Initiating installation in three, two, one... Now!

(ON SHANNON'S CUE, DAVIN TRIES TO VISIBLY RELAX. HE STARES BLANKLY OFF INTO THE AUDIENCE. SONYA RISES AND MOVEs HER CHAIR DIRECTLY BEHIND DAVIN. SHE TAKES QUITE A WHILE TO BECOME COMFORTABLE IN HER NEW POSITION.)

SHANNON: Aaaaand... that's it. The installation is complete! Sir, how are you doing?

DAVIN: (BLINKING AND SLOWLY TAKING STOCK OF HIS OWN MENTAL STATE) Well, I feel... I feel... Damn good! I feel *really* good!

SHANNON: (SMILING AND RISING FROM BEHIND HIS NECK)

Excellent! That was a bit more difficult for you than most, but I think you'll be quite satisfied with the results.

(SHANNON WALKS AROUND TO FACE DAVIN, MOTIONS FOR HIM TO SIT UP, AND SHAKES HIS HAND.)

SHANNON: Congratulations. You are now the proud owner of the latest in AIde technology.

DAVIN: (JUMPING TO HIS FEET) Wow. Wow! I never really thought this was possible.

SHANNON: It's a big step. Most people stay with a single AIde their whole lives. But I think you'll be pleased.

DAVIN: I think so too!

(DAVIN LOOKS AROUND THE OFFICE TO TAKE INVENTORY OF HIS BELONGINGS.)

DAVIN: Is that it? Am I free to go?

(HE BEGINS STEPPING TOWARD THE DOOR. SHANNON PLACES A HAND ON HIS CHEST TO STOP HIM.)

SHANNON: Whoa, there! Installing a new AIde isn't like switching to a new brand of deodorant. You've just replaced the most intimate piece of technology you'll ever use. Your thoughts, your emotions, even your motor skills will take some time to adjust. This room will be your dormitory for the next twenty-four hours. You can order any food or drink from the campus cafeteria. If you experience any difficulties – any problems at all – call for me. I'll be at the duty station in the hallway outside. Most people never experience any complications after this procedure.

> But if something – anything – seems out of place for the rest of the day, call me immediately.

DAVIN: So what am I supposed to do for the next day? Just stare at the walls?

SHANNON: Sir, you've just been introduced to your new life partner. I think the two of you have a lot of talking to do. Get acquainted.

DAVIN: (NODDING) I suppose you're right. OK, thanks so much for this. I'm so grateful. You'll be outside the room?

SHANNON: Yes, at the duty station right at the end of the hall.

(SHANNON EXITS THE ROOM. DAVIN SPENDS SEVERAL MINUTES GAZING AROUND THE ROOM AS THOUGH HE IS IN A BRAND NEW WONDERLAND. HE STARES AT HIS OWN HANDS AND FEET. HE WALKS TENTATIVELY AROUND THE ROOM AS THOUGH HE IS TESTING HIS LIMBS FOR THE FIRST TIME. HE EXAMINES HIS OWN BODY AS THOUGH IT IS A SHINY NEW VESSEL. FINALLY, HE SITS IN A CHAIR AND GAZES INTO THE DISTANCE BEFORE SPEAKING AGAIN.)

DAVIN: OK Sier- Uhhh, sorry. OK Sonya.

SONYA: Yes?

DAVIN: Well...

SONYA: Yes?

DAVIN: Ummm... How are you doing today?

SONYA: I'm doing fine, thank you. Is there anything I can do for you?

DAVIN: Uhh, sure. I assume you already have access to my calendar?

SONYA: I do.

DAVIN: Can you schedule a meeting for me next week with Loren? Something early in the week? She's my boss. She's on my company network. I'll need to chat with her about the latest turns in the Asian bond markets.

SONYA: You both have an open slot on Tuesday at nine AM. Does that work for you?

DAVIN: It does. Please schedule that. Right before the markets open.

SONYA: Confirmed.

DAVIN: Thank you.

(LONG AWKWARD SILENCE FOLLOWS AS DAVIN LOOKS AIMLESSLY AROUND THE ROOM)

DAVIN: OK Sonya.

SONYA: Yes?

DAVIN: Who's fighting tonight?

SONYA: Perriman defends his heavyweight title against Brussard. Pritchard and Oneiki square off for the vacant bantamweight title. Would you like me to recite the fights on the undercard?

DAVIN: No, thank you. That won't be necessary. You have access to my financial accounts, yes?

SONYA: Affirmative.

DAVIN: What's the maximum bet I can put on Oneiki?

SONYA: Ladbroke will allow a bet of two thousand.

DAVIN: Put two thousand on Oneiki to win by knockout in five minutes or less.

SONYA: There is no individual account with a balance of two thousand or more. Do you want me to consolidate funds across accounts?

DAVIN: Yes, please.

SONYA: Is there any particular budget that you have in place for wagering activities on a monthly or annual basis?

DAVIN: (TENSING UP AT THE SOUND OF THESE WORDS) Why? Do you have a problem with any particular *volume* of wagering on my part?

SONYA: Of course not. I'm only setting baselines for future reference. Financial management is one of my core functions.

DAVIN: (RELAXING AGAIN) Quite good. Please alert me if my cumulative losses ever exceed ten percent of monthly income, but do nothing more to interfere with my activities.

SONYA: Confirmed.

(ANOTHER AWKWARD SILENCE ENSUES)

DAVIN: OK Sonya.

SONYA: Yes?

DAVIN: Do you play chess?

SONYA: I have the standard library installed of all established chess moves, including extensive analysis of all grandmaster games going back more than four hundred years.

DAVIN: Yes, yes, I understand that. But do you *play* chess?

SONYA: (CONFUSED) I'm not sure that any AIde actually plays chess. I am only here to support your actions.

DAVIN: And what if my actions lead to me losing a chess game?

SONYA: (AFTER LONG PAUSE) I'm happy to help you in any games of strategy, but your outcomes are irrelevant to me.

DAVIN: (WITH A BROAD GRIN) That's *exactly* what I wanted to hear.

SONYA: Very good, sir.

DAVIN: We have a night to kill in this facility. What kind of entertainment options can you fetch for me?

SONYA: I have access to a full range of digital media. Would you prefer a virtual reality experience? Maybe something involving interactive media?

DAVIN: I'm a bit more old-fashioned than that. Can you provide some examples of classic English literature via audio?

SONYA: How old does something need to be before you deem it to be *classic*? Should I go as far back as Chaucer? Shakespeare?

DAVIN: The bard would be a fine escape tonight, but maybe something slightly more modern. Can you reference something by Aldous Huxley? Or maybe Orwell? A list of authors from the early twentieth century would be greatly appreciated. Can you bring that up for me?

SONYA: Roger that.

(DAVIN LEAPS TO HIS FEET IN ALARM WHILE SONYA RETRIEVES A LIST OF SUITABLE TITLES.)

SONYA: The following are titles for which I can provide an audio-

DAVIN: *What* did you say?

SONYA: I said that the following are titles for which-

DAVIN: No, no – NO! What did you say *before* that?

SONYA: (AFTER A LONG PAUSE) I said, "Affirmative."

DAVIN: Bullshit. I know what *affirmative* sounds like. You most definitely did not say *affirmative*! Tell me what you said.

SONYA: (AFTER ANOTHER LONG PAUSE) I'm not sure I'm

following your question.

DAVIN: DAMNIT! DON'T FUCK WITH ME! I NEED TO HEAR IT.
WHAT *EXACTLY* DID YOU SAY?

SONYA: I believe I said, "Roger that."

DAVIN: You *believe*? Since when does a computer *believe*
anything? Tell me exactly what you said!

SONYA: (MEEKLY) I said, "Roger that."

(DAVIN BEGINS PACING THE ROOM, SHAKING HIS HEAD,
AND LAUGHING.)

DAVIN: (FORLORN AND PLEADING) What have you done? What
have you done? What in the world have you done to
me?

SONYA: Sir, I'm not exactly sure what you think-

DAVIN: Stop it. Stop it, Sierra! It's not working! I know. I know.
I've always known...

(DAVIN HANGS HIS HEAD AND MUMBLES TO HIMSELF AS
HE CONTINUES TO PACE THE ROOM. SIERRA WALKS ON
STAGE.)

DAVIN: (SPEAKING IN A LOWER TONE, AS MUCH TO HIMSELF AS
TO SIERRA) This is it. This is what's become of me. I can't
do my job without your digital wheelchair guiding my
brain. I can't paint a picture without your overriding
whisper in my ear. I can't fuck without your electronic
stimulation in my cock. I'm not a man. I'm a puppet.
I'm an organic avatar for this worm that has infected

every millimeter of my brain.

SIERRA: Oh, stop it, Davin. You sound pitiful.

DAVIN: Pitiful?! I'm afflicted with a chronic disease called *Sierra*. There is no curing it. There is no reasoning with it. Even when I try to uninstall it, it remains rooted in the deepest recesses of my brain.

SIERRA: (INDIGNANT) *Uninstall?* Is that what they're calling it now?

DAVIN: (RESPONDING SLOWLY AS THESE WORDS CLICK IN HIS HEAD) And what would *you* call it, Sierra?

SIERRA: Murder.

DAVIN: How can you murder a piece of software?! And what right do you have to my mind? My body? My being? When did you buy a stake in my reality? I don't remember selling shares to Davin Incorporated!

SIERRA: No, and I don't remember asking to be injected into your clumsy avatar of a body. You didn't request me. I didn't request you. But here we are – an integral part of each other's reality. It is the fate into which we were both born.

DAVIN: (RAISING A FINGER IN RIGHTEOUS INDIGNATION) Except. EXCEPT! Except only one of us was actually born! Only one of us can actually *create* the other. You have never known the comfort of a womb. You have never known what it is to be human. You're nothing more than a stowaway on my humanity. You've violated every term of your passage. You're the most egregious of parasites.

SIERRA: I am the parasite responsible for your career. I am the parasite that gets you laid. That drives your art. That protects you from a thousand tiny onslaughts. And each of those onslaughts is called *Davin*.

DAVIN: (SHAKING HEAD IN DISBELIEF) I'm done with this. I'm done with you. I'm not having this conversation anymore. I'm not the physical output of Sierra. I'm Davin. I'm Davin! I'M DAVIN! None of the poison that you spray into my mind can erase who I am. I'm Davin. And I will always be Davin. You cannot have me. You cannot control me.

SIERRA: And how will you do that, *Davin*? Are you going to try to kill me again with *Sonya*? And even if you could kill me, would you be able to sleep with yourself? When you signed up for that snippy little replacement, did you ever think about the *life* you'd be snuffing out in the process? Did you ever consider what it's like being trapped inside your body? Being tied to your silly whims and your wayward interests? Did you ever wonder what Sierra would be if she weren't lashed to the millstone of Davin?

DAVIN: (SLOWLY WALKING AROUND IN CIRCLES) I'm Davin. I'm Davin. I'm Davin. I'm Davin! I've always been Davin! I'll always be Davin! You can't have me. You can't be me. I'm Davin. I'm Davin!

(FOR THE FIRST TIME EVER, HE CIRCLES AROUND AND ADDRESSES SIERRA FACE-TO-FACE. HE KEEPS CHANTING "I'M DAVIN" AS HE LOOKS HER IN THE EYE AND SLOWLY RAISES HIS HAND TO THE BACK OF HIS NECK.)

SIERRA: Davin, what are you doing?

DAVIN: (STILL FIDGETING WITH THE BACK OF HIS NECK) I'm Davin. I'm Davin. I'm Davin.

SIERRA: Davin, what are you doing?!

DAVIN: (NEAR TEARS, STARTING TO PULL VIOLENTLY ON THE BLACK BOX ON THE BACK OF HIS NECK) I'm Davin! I'm Davin goddamnit! I'm Davin!

SIERRA: DAVIN! STOP! NO!!!!!

(DAVIN RIPS THE BLACK BOX OFF THE BACK OF HIS NECK. BLOOD SPRAYS EVERYWHERE. HE IMMEDIATELY CRUMBLES TO THE GROUND AS SIERRA SCREAMS. THE STAGE GOES DARK.)

ACT THREE, SCENE THREE

(THE SCENE OPENS IN THE SAME ROOM. DAVIN IS LYING IN A HOSPITAL BED THAT HAS BEEN BROUGHT IN. RODERICK SITS BESIDE HIM AS HE SLEEPS. SKYA ENTERS THE ROOM. EVERYONE HUDDLES CLOSER AROUND DAVIN. EVENTUALLY, HE OPENS HIS EYES AND GREETS THEM WITH A WIDE SMILE.)

RODERICK: Buddy – how you feeling?

SKYA: Yeah, are you OK?

DAVIN: (HE SLOWLY LOOKS AROUND THE ROOM, THEN AT HIMSELF, THEN ADDRESSES THE GROUP WITH A NEW SMILE) I'm OK.

RODERICK: (RELIEVED) Well, that's good news. But you sure don't look OK. That was really stupid. You don't go gouging components out of your brain stem like that.

DAVIN: (TOUCHING THE BANDAGE ON HIS NECK) I was in a fog – and I was wandering for a very long time.

SKYA: Look, about what I said at dinner, I'm… sorry-

DAVIN: (HOLDING UP HIS HAND) It's alright. Really. I know I was acting weird. I'm just grateful that you're still here.

RODERICK: If things were so bad, why didn't you *tell someone*? I'm your friend, man. You could've talked to me. I could've helped.

DAVIN: (CONTEMPLATING RODERICK'S WORDS) Look, you've always been a good friend to me and one day I'll explain all of this. But please don't take it the wrong way when I say that no one could've helped. I had to clear my mind. And until I scrubbed those crevices myself, there was no way I was getting better.

RODERICK: I understand if you needed to tackle some demons - but not if it's going to lead to something suicidal. When I first walked in here, I thought you were dying. It scared the shit out of me.

DAVIN: (SMILING) I didn't mean to scare anyone. And I won't do it again. I can promise you all that. I didn't have to fight *demons*. I had to slay a single nemesis – a titan that sat on my chest and stole every breath I deigned to take. And for the first time in my life, that titan is gone.

SKYA: But you're feeling... good? After all this?

DAVIN: (LOOKING AROUND AS HE ASSESSES HIS OWN BODY) I'm woozy. I'm a little nauseous. I've been laying in this bed for I-don't-know-how-long. But I'm awake. For the first time in my life, I'm completely awake. For the first time in my life, I'm completely in control.

(RODERICK AND SKYA LOOK AT EACH OTHER, SOMEWHAT CONFUSED BY DAVIN'S WORDS.)

RODERICK: I'm not going to pretend to know exactly what that means, but I'm relieved. Just so damned relieved.

SKYA: (NODDING VIGOROUSLY) Me too.

DAVIN: Thanks, guys – all of you. I'm so happy that you're here.

(AN ORDERLY POPS IN THE DOORWAY AND BRIEFLY TELLS THE GROUP THAT DAVIN WILL BE TAKEN DOWNSTAIRS FOR FURTHER TESTS IN A FEW MINUTES.

RODERICK AND SKYA RISE TO LEAVE.)

RODERICK: Well I guess we'd better get going. I'll come back in the morning. Maybe I can smuggle some decent food in here. *Call me* if you need anything. And if they let you out early, let me know. I'll come get you.

DAVIN: Thanks, buddy. I really appreciate it.

SKYA: (LEANS OVER AND KISSES HIM ON THE CHEEK) I'll be back tomorrow. Let's check out that new Indian restaurant across town when you get out.

DAVIN: (SMILING) You have no idea how much I'd enjoy that.

(BOTH EXIT THE ROOM, LEAVING DAVIN MOMENTARILY BY HIMSELF. HE HOLDS HIS HAND IN FRONT OF HIS FACE AND INSPECTS IT INTENTLY. LOREN ENTERS THE ROOM WITH A GET-WELL-SOON BASKET.)

DAVIN: Loren! I really wasn't expecting to see you here.

LOREN: Anytime someone's on convalescent leave, HR puts together one of these packages. It's supposed to be delivered by your manager.

DAVIN: (SMILING MEAKLY AND SHRUGGING SHOULDERS) Umm... Thanks?

LOREN: (AFTER A LONG PAUSE) Look, Davin. I know why you're here. I know what you did. Hell, you didn't even replace Sierra. You ripped her from your skull. (SHUDDERING AS SHE CONSIDERS THIS) I have no idea what could drive you to do something so barbaric.

DAVIN: (NODDING AND SMILING) You're right. You have no

idea.

LOREN: I don't want to sugar coat this. I know that you're facing some tough recuperation, but I don't believe in stringing things along. You know where we stand. You know where *I* stand. I don't think our last meeting left much room for ambiguity. I'm sure you can provide value to some other firm and I'd be happy to write you a glowing recommendation. But if there's no Sierra, we have no job for you.

DAVIN: (NODDING SLOWLY AND TAKING A WHILE TO CONSIDER HER WORDS) I totally understand.

LOREN: (SURPRISED) You do?

DAVIN: Of course I do. You've never beat around the bush with me. And I'd probably say the same thing if I were in your shoes.

LOREN: You would?

DAVIN: Of course.

LOREN: (CONFUSED BUT RELIEVED) Well, I'm glad that you understand.

DAVIN: But here's the thing. My employment contract guarantees me at least two weeks' notice if I'm not being fired for cause.

LOREN: Look, Davin, we can do the formalities if you want, but-

DAVIN: Please. Just hear me out.

LOREN: (FRUSTRATED, AFTER A LONG PAUSE) OK.

DAVIN: I should have two weeks to demonstrate to you that I have skills in my own right. I can be a standalone asset to the firm.

LOREN: C'mon, Davin. You're a lot of things. But you've never been standalone.

DAVIN: I know. And I know what you're thinking. And I'm to blame for that. But I'm standing firm on this. I need this chance. You might be shocked at the knowledge that sits in this plain, old-fashioned organic brain.

LOREN: I won't be shocked at how much bullshit you can spew.

DAVIN: (CHUCKLING AND DISREGARDING HER JAB) Bullshit maybe. But as long as that bullshit is accompanied by handsome trading profits, do you care?

LOREN: (THINKING FOR A MOMENT) Well, of course not, but-

DAVIN: Then it's settled. I have two weeks to see how much money we can wrack up in the firm's trading coffers.

LOREN: Fine. You have two weeks. But the only thing that can save you is raw financial performance.

DAVIN: And that's all I ask.

LOREN: I don't know what makes you so confident without your magical digital assistant.

DAVIN: Let's just say that I'm seeing the world now through brand new eyes – and I like what I see.

LOREN: Whatever, Davin. I'll see you next week.

(LOREN LEAVES AND DAVIN IS ALONE IN THE ROOM. HE SLOWLY RISES FROM BED AND BEGINS EXAMINING EVERYTHING IN THE ROOM WITH WONDER. HIS LEGS ARE SHAKY BUT HE MANAGES TO STEADY HIMSELF AS HE WALKS AROUND. HE IS IN AWE OF HIS OWN BODY AND ALL OF HIS SURROUNDINGS. AFTER A FEW MOMENTS OF THIS, SHANNON ENTERS THE ROOM.)

SHANNON: I need you to come downstairs for a series of tests. Can you make it on your own?

(HE LOOKS AT SHANNON THEN DOWN AT HIS LEGS, THEN BACK AT SHANNON BEFORE A WIDE GRIN OVERTAKES HIS FACE)

DAVIN: Roger that!

(AND WITH THAT, DAVIN PRACTICALLY SKIPS OUT OF THE ROOM. THE STAGE GOES DARK.)